Beck hurried to catch Barrabas

If he hadn't been in such a hurry, he would have seen the pothole. If he had seen the pothole, he wouldn't have fallen flat on his face directly in front of the Russian tank.

He rolled onto his back, gasping, trying to catch his breath, which had rushed from his lungs when he'd landed.

The huge iron monster had awakened.

The 780-horsepower diesels roared and the tank lurched forward on its twelve wheels and double tracks. It was a nightmare come to life. The nose of the tank loomed over him, shutting off the light of the stars. The earth shook beneath him as the treads supporting the fifty tons of metal rolled onward. The underside of the tank's hull covered him. Smothered him. Beck was about to be crushed, mangled by the tracks, sucked up into the grinding drive wheels. Or if Barrabas shot a rocket to halt the advancing killing machine, he'd be trapped in the fiery explosion.

Nate Beck was about to die.

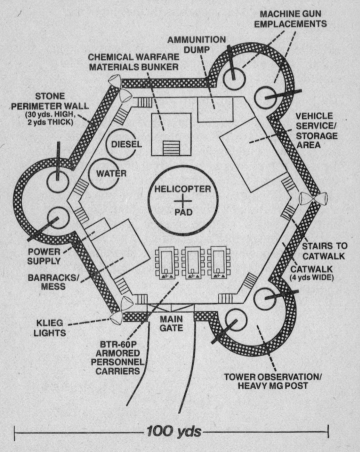

CHEMICAL WARFARE STOCKPILE
SOVIET MILITARY GARRISON
OUTSIDE KABUL, AFGHANISTAN
(CONVERTED 16TH CENTURY MOGUL STONE FORT)

MACHINE GUN EMPLACEMENTS

AMMUNITION DUMP

CHEMICAL WARFARE MATERIALS BUNKER

STONE PERIMETER WALL
(30 yds. HIGH, 2 yds THICK)

VEHICLE SERVICE/ STORAGE AREA

DIESEL

WATER

HELICOPTER PAD

STAIRS TO CATWALK

CATWALK (4 yds WIDE)

POWER SUPPLY

BARRACKS/ MESS

KLIEG LIGHTS

MAIN GATE

BTR-60P ARMORED PERSONNEL CARRIERS

TOWER OBSERVATION/ HEAVY MG POST

— 100 yds —

SOBs

JIHAD

JACK HILD

A GOLD EAGLE BOOK FROM

WORLDWIDE

TORONTO • NEW YORK • LONDON • PARIS
AMSTERDAM • STOCKHOLM • HAMBURG
ATHENS • MILAN • TOKYO • SYDNEY

When you are wounded and left on the Afghanistani
    plains
And the women come out to cut up what remains,
Just roll to your rifle and blow out your brains
And go to your god like a soldier.

—Rudyard Kipling

Shoravi Padar Lanath!

—An Afghani saying

First edition May 1986

ISBN 0-373-61612-0

Special thanks and acknowledgment to
Alan Philipson for his contributions to this work.

Printed in Canada

1

Aziz Khan scrambled on all fours up the winding goat path. A meter to his left, the weathered granite mountainside dropped off abruptly. It was nearly a 750-meter straight fall to the canyon valley below, a wedge of green hidden between the rugged peaks of the Afghanistan high desert. If he had looked down, Aziz could have seen his village, a little cluster of mud-walled houses surrounded by fields of wheat. He did not look down. Aziz clutched for handholds among the boulders and loose rubble, choking on puffs of rock dust raised by the heels of his friend, Tajik Bula.

For as long as he could remember, Aziz had been able to outrun Tajik. In the past three months the other teenager had grown six inches in height, almost all of it in the legs, with no accompanying gain in weight. Now Tajik, a spindly scarecrow in baggy, shapeless pants, taunted Aziz with strides the latter could not hope to match.

"How much farther?" he called to the boy's back.

Tajik Bula glanced over his shoulder, giving Aziz a quick glimpse of profile: the long, sharply hooked nose, the sparse, downy fuzz on a receding chin and the black laughing eyes. Instead of answering the question, Tajik picked up the pace.

As Aziz fell farther behind, he mentally kicked himself for being such a fool. He should have known better than to follow Tajik up the mountain. For one thing, he had been forbidden to associate with the boy anymore; for another, he had left his farm chores half done. What irritated him the most was how easily Tajik had manipulated him, alternately tantalizing and badgering him with hints about a secret both dangerous and wonderful. At age fourteen, Aziz Khan could stand cold, he could stand hunger and pain, but he could not yet stand not knowing. The sooner he found out what surprise Tajik had in store, the sooner he could return home to face the certainty of his father's wrath.

The gap between the two boys grew until Aziz was climbing alone. Then he rounded a tight turn and found Tajik Bula sitting on a fallen slab of granite, waiting, legs crossed, pants cuffs up around his bony shins.

"So there you are," Tajik said, a broad smile on his face. "I had begun to think you'd turn coward and gone back to your ditch-digging."

Flushed, panting from exertion, Aziz tightly clenched his fists. Never content with his mischief, Tajik Bula always had to give the pot one more stir. Making trouble for others was a trait Aziz's father said ran in the Bula family, passed down through the generations like an heirloom prayer rug. The village mullah was of the same opinion.

"Is this the place?" Aziz demanded. "What do you have to show me?"

"Wouldn't you like to guess first?"

Aziz had had enough. Whatever the surprise was, it wasn't worth further humiliation. He would not beg to see it. He about-faced at once and started back down the mountain.

"No, wait!" Tajik said, hopping off his seat. "Don't go!"

Aziz stopped only when the other boy clapped a hand on his shoulder.

"It was a game. I was only teasing," Tajik told him. "I'll show you."

Tajik hurried back to the slab of granite, then slipped behind it. He disappeared completely for a second. When he stepped out, he held a long flat parcel wrapped in oiled paper and tied with twine. He set it down carefully on the flat rock.

Aziz recognized the type of wrapping immediately. A gun. Tajik had a gun. He ran up for a closer look.

The boy untied the string and folded the paper back.

Not just any gun. A black gun.

Anger, chores and father were instantly forgotten.

"Avtomat Kalashnikov!" Aziz exclaimed as his friend proudly held the Soviet-made assault rifle across his narrow chest.

Since the Russian invasion of their country in December 1979, Aziz and Tajik, like other Afghan boys, had played the invader-mujahedeen game. From the age of nine, they'd used sticks for their rifles, rocks for grenades, and the strong boys had always got to be mujahedeen, "holy warriors." The mullah had taught the valley people they should not put their faith in man-made weapons, that victory against the Soviet invaders depended on Allah alone. Be that as it may, the gun that Tajik clutched was most surely the weapon of weapons, a symbol of power in a raped land. And this particular gun was brand-new; not a single scratch marred its flat black finish.

Tajik released the magazine catch tab and stripped away the 30-round banana clip, showing Aziz the bright brass of the top two live cartridges in the staggered-row box magazine.

"How did you get it?"

Tajik puffed out his chest. "I killed a *Shoravi* and took it from his dead hands."

"*You* killed a Russian?"

Tajik basked for a moment in his friend's astonishment, then reinserted the magazine and rocked it back into place. "I stabbed him with my knife," he said, shouldering the nine-pound rifle and sighting across the valley at a distant peak.

Aziz frowned. Among other things, Tajik Bula was a well-known teller of tall tales. Except for the evidence of the black gun, this had all the earmarks of one of his stories. Bravery certainly had never been one of Tajik's attributes, even in play war. And killing an AK-armed Russian with a knife was the deed of a *ghazi*, an Islamic warrior, something every devout, patriotic Afghan, boy and man, aspired to become.

"Two nights ago, on the way back from Kabul, I nearly stepped into the path of a *Shoravi* foot patrol," the taller boy said. "I got back to cover before they saw me. After they passed along the road I followed for more than five kilometers, keeping to the darkness and shadows. Then one of them dropped out of line to relieve himself at the side of the road. It was so dark I could barely see him. I waited until I heard his pee hitting the ground. Then I rushed him from the side and hit him in the head with a piece of rock. At the last second he saw me coming, but I was too fast."

"But you said you stabbed him?"

"I did, I did. After I hit him with the rock. I rolled him into the ditch beside the road and…" He lowered the captured rifle and brusquely swept his index finger across his throat from ear to ear.

"The rest of the patrol didn't come back after him?"

"I don't know. I took the gun and I ran."

Aziz didn't know what to believe. Except the running part—that definitely sounded like Tajik. Yet the proof was there, in the other boy's hands. Hard as it was to swallow, Tajik had killed a Russian and taken his gun. He was a hero of Islam, certain to die without pain and to ascend straight to heaven.

"Soon I will leave the village and go to the mountain caves of the mujahedeen," Tajik said. "I will join the other warriors and help them drive the Soviet donkeys from our land."

Aziz still had some questions. "Why did you hide the gun? Why did you hide your bravery from everyone?"

"I feared for my family's safety. There might be reprisals against them if the news got out to agents of Khad." He referred to the KGB-trained Afghan Secret Police.

"Khad in our village?"

"They are everywhere."

Aziz doubted the reprisal story. Their valley was too isolated and insignificant to interest Khad, even though the farmers were supplying the mujahedeen with small quantities of food. In fact, only twice since the Soviet invasion had government MiG 21s tried to low-altitude bomb their fields and houses. Both times little or no damage had been done. The village wasn't worth a full-scale air strike.

The true nature of Tajik's dilemma over the gun, Aziz realized, had more to do with the Bulas than the Russians or their lackeys in Kabul. The AK was worth almost two thousand U.S. dollars on the black market. If Tajik showed the gun to his family, they would take it away from him and sell it and he would never get to use it in battle.

"If I'd had more time to work on that *khal*," Tajik said, grinning, "I'd have skinned him alive. Starting from the soles of his feet—"

A noise interrupted the string of hollow boasts. A droning from the southwest. "Planes?" Tajik said as the droning grew louder.

Aziz pointed across the canyon, at a saddle between two peaks. "There!"

Not planes—helicopters. Soviet gunships: MI-24 Hinds, painted kelly green and lemon yellow camouflage, bristling with rocket pods and cannon. An entire battle wing swept over the saddle and dropped into the valley. The angry throb of rotor blades rebounded off the sheer canyon walls, echoing reechoing, melding into an indistinguishable roar.

Never had the village looked so small to Aziz Khan.

Never had he felt so helpless.

The Hinds flew low and tight, in attack formation, their long shadows gliding over rotorwash-whipped green fields. Aziz did not want to watch, but he could not tear his gaze away. He saw the rocket pods of the lead gunships wink and puff smoke. A split second later he heard the pop of their firing. Rockets screamed the length of the valley, impacting the village dead center. The mud buildings did not blow up. Instead they burst into rolling clouds of yellowish gas that obscured everything. The people and animals that ran into the swirling smoke seemed to disappear. If there were screams, they were smothered by the whump of multiple detonations, the whine of gunship turbines.

Aziz saw his own house take a direct hit. Tears spilled down his cheeks and he could not breathe. His mother and sisters were in there, baking bread. His father and brothers were working in the field beyond, a field now veiled by yellow fog. A field where by rights he should have been.

"Shoot them!" he shrieked at Tajik. "Use the black gun! Shoot them!"

Tajik had slipped to his knees, into a posture of Muslim prayer. He seemed to be paralyzed with shock and horror; his eyes and mouth were wide open, his skin deathly pale.

Aziz did not hesitate. He jumped for the gun, sobbing as he wrenched it from Tajik's stiff, lifeless grasp. He cracked back the AK's actuating handle and let it snap forward, chambering round number one, then depressed the safety/fire-selector switch. He shouldered the rifle, tracking the foremost gunship, then pinned the trigger back. *"Allah e akbar!"* he screamed over the staccato clatter of full-automatic fire. As the action spat shell casings, the buttstock buffeted him savagely, wildly shifting the point of aim.

"No! No, stop!" Tajik yelled in his ear. "They haven't seen us yet!"

Aziz let go his death squeeze on the trigger. Not because of Tajik's warning. He couldn't hold the weapon on target while he fired sustained full-auto. He quickly fisted the tears from his eyes so he could see the front sight post, then grimly resumed, three rounds at a time. The short bursts still raised the AK's muzzle, but not enough to completely throw off his aim.

Suddenly the lead gunship swung out of formation, banking toward them, climbing rapidly. Aziz had finally gotten their attention.

"Run!" Tajik howled, vaulting up the trail. He dived for cover behind the flat slab of rock.

Aziz kept shooting as the gunship raced upward, holding the sights more or less on the flash of reflected sun on the Hind's windscreen. He shot until the firing pin snapped on an empty chamber; only then did he run after Tajik. Cannon fire pulverized the granite outcrops, sending shudders up through the bottoms of his feet all the way to his hips. Sizzling bits of rock ricocheted into the exposed backs of his legs as he squirmed to cover. Rotorwash slammed the boys, blinding them with dust as the gunship wheeled away to make a second pass.

On his belly under the flat rock, his nose buried in the dirt, hands clamped over his ears, eyes tightly shut, Aziz prayed aloud for the safety of his family. Beside him beneath the stone, at an even greater volume Tajik Bula was praying as well, but only for himself.

DR. HERMANN ULM'S STOMACH lurched up into his throat as the MI-24 gunship power-dived into the valley, a screaming four-hundred-meter drop. He swallowed a huge gulp of air and, gritting his teeth, held the gullet-splitting bubble down, his rubber-gloved fingers digging deep into the cushioned armrests of the copilot's seat. The attack helicopter leveled out ten meters from the valley floor, engine howling, g-force times three driving the blood from his brain.

For a terrible instant his vision went black around the edges, tunneling out. He had to concentrate with all his strength to keep from fainting. As heavy and uncomfortable as his gas mask was, he was grateful for the concealment it provided. It completely covered his head from the neck up. Only his eyes and upper cheeks showed through the mask's two gogglelike glass view ports. The Soviet gunship crew, likewise attired, could not see and take pleasure in his panic and fear. The wave of dizziness began to ebb as they closed on their target. Dr. Ulm stifled the urge to check his fluttering pulse. He knew he wouldn't be able to find it under the butyl gauntlets, hooded butyl long coat and the specially treated, chemically impermeable undergarment.

This was not a job for an old man, but it was a job this old man had stubbornly refused to delegate. A professional research scientist for more than forty-five years, Dr. Ulm knew there was no such thing as a perfect experiment, even inside a laboratory. Today's trial was perfect in its imperfection, a true test of Soman II, the crowning achievement of his life, in a totally uncontrolled microenvironment. It was something he could not bear to miss, even if it killed him.

He noted the wind's speed and direction as registered on the MI-24's instruments. It was gusting eleven knots from the north-northeast, almost at right angles to the line of attack. It couldn't have been better for the purposes of the experiment. In the enclosed canyon, he would get an accurate picture of the all-important dispersal rate. The design of an efficient gas weapon delivery system was an extremely complicated business, a delicate juggling of particle size, fluid density, explosive package power and maximum crosswind velocity. This field trial was a calibration exercise, the quantity measured being human deaths per square meter.

The Russian pilot beside him raised a gauntleted right hand to gas-masked neck, squeezed his throat microphone and barked the command to fire. The Hind shuddered beneath Ulm as its rockets launched en masse. A flock of metal-skinned banshees streaked away, their exhaust trails cutting a ruler line to the village's crude central square.

Ulm could not suppress a shout of exhultation as the low-powered dispersal warheads burst on target. Soman II, as yellow as blooming daffodils, materialized out of nothing, rapidly spreading from the rocket-impact points in mingling cottony masses. In the trailing gunships, high-speed infrared cameras were busy recording the height, speed and volume of the billowing gas clouds.

Ulm watched in fascination as people and farm animals running along the edge of the opaque mist dropped in their tracks, felled by the razor-keen blade of his genius. Though it was a sight he had witnessed literally hundreds of thousands of times during his long career, it never failed to stir his blood. The cameras watched, too, probing deeply into the yellow fog with their heat-sensitive film, making it possible to later precisely time the minute intervals between exposure to Soman II and incapacitation.

The lead gunship bore down on the smoke-shrouded village, climbing as it did so to avoid passing directly through the deadly gas. Something rattled against the Hind's roof on the doctor's side. A quick flurry of hail. Steel-cored hail.

The copilot, who had vacated his usual chair so the honored observer might have the best possible view, sagged on the fold-down jump seat, slipped to his knees on the metal deck, arms hanging limply at his sides. There was a hole the size of a dime through the right top of his gas-masked head, well above and behind the line of his ear. He crumpled, twisting to face the cabin and Dr. Ulm as he toppled to his side. The left lens of his mask's goggles was gone, blown out by the exiting slug. Blood pulsed from the ruin of his eye socket, washing bits of brain and bone down the corrugated hose of his rebreather unit and onto the floor.

More bullets pelted the gunship's tail section.

"Incoming! Incoming!" the two surviving crew members croaked into their throat mikes.

The pilot responded, veering up and banking sharply.

"What are you doing?" Ulm demanded. "Why are you breaking off?"

"We are under fire," the Russian snarled back. "I am taking appropriate retaliatory action."

Ulm wanted to make a further protest but found he could not. The full-power climb was too steep, too fast; it pressed him hard into his seat. It felt as if someone or something enormous was sitting in the middle of his chest; it was all he could do to inhale.

"I see the *basmachi*," the pilot said.

The doctor strained but could see nothing but rock and precariously perched, stunted pines. Then something flickered from above. The muzzle-flash of a Kalashnikov.

A slug plowed through the center of the windscreen, passing between Ulm and the pilot, whining the length of the gunship. The doctor stared at the round, crusty hole. Wind whistled through it— a shrill, sour note.

The small-arms' fire stopped just before the Hind came level with the goat trail. The pilot swooped his gunship down on a madly running figure. It was skinny and small. A child in rags. Carrying an assault rifle.

Cannon roared.

All around the weaving, darting figure the ground was instantly chewed to hell. Cannon rounds sparked off rock, kicking up plumes of dust.

"Get him! Get the little bastard!" one of the crew shouted above the din, clinging to the back of the copilot's seat and peering over Dr. Ulm's shoulder.

Then the small figure ducked behind a flat granite slab.

The pilot broke off the frontal attack, circled and came in from a different, higher angle. Hovering, he poured cannon fire onto the top of the flat rock, pocking the stone with white craters. The savagely concentrated fire had no effect on the integrity of the cover. It did, however, shake the mountainside enough to start an avalanche from the trail above. Tons of rubble poured down, burying the site.

The Soviet pilot dropped for a closer look, rotorwash blowing back the obscuring clouds of dust. The flat rock was no longer visible under the slide of boulders and rotten rock.

"Two hundred rounds of cannon fire to kill one little boy," Dr. Ulm mused aloud.

"He killed one of my crew," the pilot snapped back.

Dr. Ulm ignored the protest. "If you are satisfied, if you have wasted enough time and ammunition on your most worthy adversary, perhaps you'd be good enough to take me down to the valley floor, where I'm supposed to be. Upwind of the gas, if you don't mind."

The pilot obeyed, putting the Hind into another bowel-wrenching dive. Ulm closed his eyes and clawed at the armrests. He didn't open them until he felt the helicopter's skids touch solid ground.

Three other Hinds had also landed in the wheat field; the remaining gunships circled overhead, filming the aftermath and the continuing windward spread of Soman II.

Ulm got out of the helicopter and started walking across the field toward the village square. He turned on his tape recorder and activated his throat mike. It was slow going in the chemwar suit, slow and hot. The rest of the research team was already at work. He could see them photographing and turning over bodies ahead.

He hurried, though it increased his discomfort. It wasn't just that he was afraid he was missing some important discovery; Dr. Ulm felt a proprietary interest in the village full of new corpses. He had created them. The were *his*. By the time he reached the others he was sweating profusely inside the protective suit. Perspiration trickled steadily down the back of his neck, down the undersides of his arms, pooling in the fingertips of his gloves.

His Soviet research assistants were examining the body of a young Afghan woman. They had cut away her *chadri*, the traditional all-concealing, head-to-toe garment for Muslim women, and slit away her undergarments, as well. She lay naked on her back in the dirt.

Ulm shouldered his way into the huddle for a closer look. Bright yellow droplets, the consistency of motor oil, were clustered around the dead girl's nose and eyes. Her face was the color of beetroot, cheek muscles locked tight, lips peeled back. On her mouth, chin and clenched teeth, blood was smeared. In her death throes she had bitten off the end of her tongue.

One of the assistants turned to Dr. Ulm and made a hand gesture, as if zipping himself up from crotch to forehead. Ulm nodded. A body bag was in order. She had fallen at the outermost perimeter of the gas and was, therefore, a prime candidate for careful dissection.

Ulm continued on through the field, moving quickly from corpse to corpse, noting in his tape recorder anything unusual about the position or condition of the bodies, the amount of gas residue clinging to outer clothing and surrounding wheat stalks. Each of the victims would be given an identification number by the research team and, with the aid of aerial photographs, assigned a place on the kill-zone overlay grid. The coordinates of every individual death would eventually be fed into a computer along with corresponding measurements of Soman II concentration and droplet size.

The doctor entered the village proper, ground zero, exactly fourteen minutes after detonation. Yellow chemical slime lay in puddles in the open earthen gutters, in the ruts in the unpaved streets. It clung to the walls of the mud buildings like paint spatters. People and animals lay scattered everywhere. Mounds of them. All were sprinkled with the sticky yellow rain. All were dead.

Ulm bypassed the unprotected victims and made straight for the nearest mud house off the square with a closed front door and sealed windows. The door was unlocked; he pushed it open and looked in.

A family of nine—toddlers, teenagers, mother, father, grandparents—was sprawled on and around the rough-hewn table. They had been about to eat their midday meal. They now lay amid it.

Ulm immediately checked the windowsills. With the naked eye, he could detect no tiny yellow droplets. Likewise, he checked the door. There was no evidence of Soman II. Puzzled, he turned back to the room. Death had been so sudden that none of the victims had managed to get more than a step away from the table. For that to have happened

Ulm knew there had to be a substantial amount of liquefied nerve agent in the room. The fireplace, he thought—that had to have been the entry point. He knelt on the hearth, bending low to examine the single splatter of yellow the size of a man's thumb-nail that had fallen through the chimney onto the bed of ash and cinders. It was more than enough.

Tears came to his eyes as he rose to his feet. He was overcome by the perfection of his own crea-tion. Hermann Ulm had no love for Russia or Russians, but when it came to funding and re-search priorities, he had found them infinitely su-perior to his former bosses in the Third Reich.

Before the war he had worked as a junior biochemist at I. G. Farben under Dr. Gerhard Schrader. In a search for a better insecticide, they had uncovered a new family of nerve poisons, ace-tylcholine-esterase (ACHE) inhibitors, which made a living body unable to stop its nerve firings, caus-ing it to literally strangle in the spasms of its own organs.

This monumental discovery had meant little to the Nazi party bureaucrats and pencil pushers who controlled the wartime checkbook. They were ner-vous about such weapons, afraid of Allied coun-terattacks in kind. The ACHE program was put on the back burner in favor of the development of a cheap, reliable chemical agent for use in the death camps. As far as Ulm was concerned, the Zyclon B

project was distinguished only by its crudity. The SS
wanted a product that was safe for untrained personnel to handle and one that could be manufac-
tured quickly and in quantity. The chemistry
involved could have been successfully tackled by a
bright twelve-year-old—no ingenuity, no challenge.

Because of his experience with gas weapons, Ulm
was inducted into the SS Death's Head Corps and
performed his military service at Treblinka. There
he oversaw the murder of two hundred thousand
people with Zyclon B and carbon monoxide. He
found the routine of camp life boring. He considered the job of helping to keep a vast killing machine operational to be unworthy of his talents.

In 1945, outside Berlin, Ulm was captured by the
Red Army. He spent a year in a Soviet prison camp
under a fictitious name. When his true identity and
wartime job were discovered, he thought he was
going to be executed on the spot. Instead, he was
put back to work on gas warfare projects for the
U.S.S.R., with a bigger budget, his own laboratory and assistants.

For forty years he had lived the life of a ballet
star or champion athlete. He had his own car, his
own apartment in close proximity to other former
Nazi scientists with whom he exclusively social-
ized. He had made no conversion to the tenets of
Marx and Lenin and had not been pressed to do so.

Dr. Hermann Ulm had, in short, not only escaped punishment for his crimes against humanity, he had also been richly rewarded for them.

His greatest reward was yet to come.

Ulm carefully, almost reverently backed out of the shabby room full of the freshly dead. He now had the scientific proof he needed to convince his superiors in Kabul that Soman II was the key to breaking the back of the mujahedeen resistance, the key to the destruction of their otherwise impregnable mountain-cave sanctuaries.

Dr. Hermann Ulm was going to win the war in Afghanistan all by himself.

AZIZ KHAN FELT THE RUMBLE of the landslide just before it struck. Instinctively, he drew his legs up tight under him and held his breath. The noise was earsplitting. Everything shook beneath the flat rock. The lighter things shook the most. He was among those things. His body bounced between the earth and the underside of great stone. He clung to the dirt with all his might.

Pressure slammed his eardrums as the air was driven out from under the rock. Then the shaking stopped. He opened his eyes and could see nothing for the dust. The darkness was suffocating. Lungs burning, he sipped at the air and fell into a violent coughing jag.

He could hear Tajik coughing as well, coughing and crying.

His eyes streaming tears, Aziz blinked away the grit and turned under the stone, turned to face the way he had crawled in. All was black. He felt with his hands and found a wall of tightly packed rock. He could not shift any of the stones. Panic rose in his throat. He fought it down with prayer.

Then his hand hit the ragged end of a tree branch. He pulled on it and it moved. He twisted it from side to side and a ray of light cut into the darkness. Using the branch as a lever he opened a hole in the rockfall. He shoved his head out and breathed deeply, giving thanks to Allah.

After he cleared away a hole big enough to crawl through, he went back for Tajik. The boy was trembling with fear and had to be half dragged to safety. Aziz helped his friend through the opening and left him gasping for air while he returned to the flat rock one last time.

"You almost forgot this," he said, slithering through the hole, holding the black gun out in front of him.

Tajik's eyes widened in horror. For a second, Aziz thought the boy was going to scream. Tajik jerked his gaze away from the AK and stared down at the ruin of their village. Some of the helicopters had landed, and Soviet personnel were milling in the fields. There were no villagers moving.

Aziz could see that his prayers had been for nothing; his family was lost. "It's going to be all right," Aziz said, swallowing his own anguish. One of them had to be strong if they were going to survive. "We'll go up into the mountains and join the mujahedeen. We'll make the Russian donkeys pay for what they have done today. We will have *badal*, blood for blood. Here, take your gun."

Tajik began to sob into his palms.

"Come on, my friend," Aziz said soothingly. "Get up and let's see if you can walk. We have a long way to go."

2

Walker Jessup set his fiberglass cafeteria tray on the stainless steel gurney. He stared wistfully at the precariously balanced heap of plates, dishes, bowls and cups he had personally licked clean; for Jessup the memory of food consumed was invariably bittersweet. Heaving an almost inaudible sigh, he turned and lumbered back across the U.S. Department of Commerce basement-level cafeteria. He drew a fresh tray and set of utensils from the bins and entered the serving line, which was all but deserted. He passed by the various cold salads, juices and hors d'oeuvres, sliding his empty tray over chromed rails.

The black lady in charge of sandwiches brought her fifteen-inch carving knife to port arms when she saw him coming "You again?" she said.

Over the maple syrup of piped-in music, Jessup could plainly hear her toe tapping, not in time to the all-string rendition of "Moon River," but in irritation. The stick-thin woman was practically defying him to place another order.

Jessup found himself mildly amused. An old hand at Washington fun and games, the former CIA operative was accustomed to hypocrisy, at all levels of government service. The hypocrisy in question had to do with appetite. There was a fine line of difference, it seemed, between a "healthy" and an "unhealthy" desire to feed. The difference was the ability to metabolize what one consumed. It was perfectly all right, even laudable, to eat like a ravening swine as long as it didn't show. On Jessup it showed. All over. The Texan weighed in the neighborhood of 350 pounds, stripped. Though he was a tall man and broadly built across the shoulders, he still looked like the Goodyear blimp in a sports jacket.

"I'll have," Jessup drawled with ponderous dignity, "a pair of the rare roast beef sandwiches, dipped, on kaiser rolls with the works."

The sandwich lady rolled her eyes in disgust.

Jessup could not resist. "And a large bowl of the bean soup with extra crackers."

The woman muttered something to the cold cuts that he could not make out.

With much unnecessary clattering of cutlery and banging of plates, the sandwich lady eventually hurled Jessup's order at his tray.

"I'm cutting you off, mister," she told him as he slid his goodies away. "That's the last you get from me today, hear?"

Jessup bore his cross and his tray over to the dessert counter for a slice of cream-topped pumpkin pie and a couple of chocolate éclairs. He stopped at the soft drink dispenser on the way to the cash register. He almost took a giant-size diet soda. Almost. In for a penny, he told himself, filling the forty-ounce cup to overflowing with regular cola.

The D.C. lunchtime crowd had left the cafeteria. Jessup weaved his way around and between the littered tables to a little alcove separated from the main dining area by a brown vinyl accordion room divider.

The senator's private secretary pretended not to notice Jessup as he set his tray down on the table. She was busy buffing her two-inch-long fingernails, painted screaming red to match her wet-look lipstick. She pursed her full, pouty mouth as she worked.

"I brought an extra sandwich in case either of you were hungry," the Texan said politely as he removed the various dishes from the tray.

The senator shook his bald and blotchy head.

"How about you, miss?" Jessup pushed the plate toward her, causing a rivulet of beef juice to slop onto and across the table. It missed the elbow of her fuzzy pink cashmere sweater by a good six inches.

The brunette secretary glanced at the fatty, dripping sandwich, then glared up at the fat, grinning man. From her expression he might well have just offered her a case of AIDS. She rose from the table. "I have some work to do in the office, if you don't need me here, sir," she said. Without waiting for a reply from her boss, she slipped her purse over her shoulder and made a hip-swinging exit.

Jessup winced at glutei maximi rolling together under the tight pink skirt like precision gears. The senator knew how to pick them, all right.

By feel.

The senator had a new girl every time Jessup saw him. And no wonder. He paid them thirty thousand a year, with no typing, no filing, no phones. All he asked was that they occasionally indulge an old man's harmless whims. As Jessup sat down the lawmaker backed his motorized wheelchair away from the table and, with a violent twist of the control lever, sent it lurching forward.

Jessup had to move his foot or lose it. He expected no apology from the little man in the black mortician's suit and string tie. He was not disappointed.

"The committee met yesterday," the senator told him. "We have a project in mind."

"The committee" had nothing to do with the Senate. It wasn't an official government body. Though secretly funded through tax dollars, it was not subject to the same checks and balances as the other branches of the system. Something that did not exist could not be monitored. The business of the committee was pain and suffering. Pain and suffering for the enemies of the United States who could not otherwise be hurt, owing to restrictions by international treaty or law. The committee financed small, neat military operations that could not be linked to any segment of the U.S. Armed Forces. Walker Jessup was an independent contractor, a middleman with his own private international intelligence network. Known as "the Fixer" in the trade, he arranged for certain people to be in certain places at certain times and made sure they had access to appropriate hardware.

Jessup picked up his first sandwich in both hands, licked his lips and said, "Where?"

"Afghanistan."

Jessup set the roast beef back on the plate, untouched. He wiped his mouth with a paper napkin and said, "Six figures."

"But you don't know what the mission is yet!"

"Don't know and don't care. The Soldiers of Barrabas won't cross into Soviet-controlled territory again for less than six figures per man. Take it or leave it."

The senator's eyes glittered nastily above his half glasses. They both knew he had to take it. "Shall I explain the program?"

Jessup nodded.

"The Russian stalemate in Afghanistan is about to be broken. Undoubtedly you've heard the rumors about the introduction of chemical weapons into the conflict."

"You mean 'yellow rain'? I heard that was a CIA propaganda scam. Turned out to be some kind of tropical bee shit."

"This isn't bee shit. This is a new refinement of Soman."

"The nerve gas."

"Only more lethal by a factor of one thousand. We have hard evidence that a large quantity of the material has been moved to a secure storage area outside Kabul. It is about to be used against the mujahedeen mountain strongholds that even Spetsnaz have been unable to take."

"If they use nerve gas in a major assault, word is bound to leak out to the world press."

"The Russians don't care about public opinion," the senator said. "They're losing the war, and this is a quick way to end it."

"What's the mission objective?"

"The committee wants the Kabul storage depot sabotaged before the gas can be used against the rebels."

"And?"

The senator smiled. "The committee wants to put a permanent halt to this particular thrust of the

Soviet gas warfare program. It wants the sabotage to look like a major failure in system design. An accident of tragic proportions."

Jessup scowled down at the little lawmaker. "If the stockpile is as big as you make out, we're not talking about tragedy, here; we're talking about genocide."

"Pick up the file this afternoon. How you choose to get the job done is your business. The committee isn't fussy." Having said his piece, the senator motored away.

The committee was never fussy, Jessup thought blackly as he looked at his food. He prodded the pumpkin pie with a fork. It quivered like rubber under the tines. His appetite gone, Jessup pushed the plate away. He knew Colonel Barrabas would need no coaxing to take on this job. The Afghan mission had the three elements the white-haired mercenary leader found irresistible.

It was high paying.

It was dirty.

And it was almost impossible.

3

Nile Barrabas stripped off his worn British G.I.-issue sweater and threw it on an equally threadbare sofa. Under the sweater he wore nothing but his own skin. He shivered involuntarily.

"Chilly, are we?" the black-haired woman said as she opened her medical bag. "That'll teach you to move to such a godforsaken spot."

"I like it here," Barrabas said.

Dr. Leona Hatton took out a stethoscope. "This is what passes for summer here, remember. Wait till winter and then tell me about it."

Barrabas glanced at the stone cottage's small windows. Bright July sunlight streamed through them, and through myriad cracks in putty and frames whistled a stiff wind straight off the Atlantic, which was only four miles from the front door. From where he stood Barrabas could see the expanse of gentle slope leading down to the small Cornish seacoast village of Tintagel, a tilted plain of gorse and fern that ended abruptly in a long straight drop to the ocean. On the landward side of his cottage, the slope rose another four miles to meet the rocky ridge top of a low mountain.

If there was nothing to stop the wind, there was also no way a hostile force of any size could move unnoticed against his position. The former U.S. Army colonel was not a paranoiac; he was a pure realist. In his career as a professional soldier, he had made more enemies than he could count. Even though he was thought in many circles to be dead, there was always a chance of discovery. His little stone house had withstood the elements for four hundred years. Short of an aerial or artillery bombardment, it would stand for four hundred more.

"Take the pants off, too," Dr. Hatton instructed him. "We both agreed this is to be a complete physical."

"Sounds more like a thin excuse to get me naked."

Lee Hatton laughed and shook her head. She wore her hair close-cropped, like a man's. Instead of detracting from her beauty, the austere hairstyle emphasized it, drawing attention to her large dark eyes and full-lipped mouth. "I'm an MD," she reminded him. "I have the ethics of my profession to consider. Not to mention the fact that I don't need an excuse like that to get you stripped down to your birthday suit. A short whistle would suffice."

"Or you could just snap your fingers," he suggested, as he dropped his trousers.

"Sit," she ordered, pointing at the sofa.

The randy banter was just play. They both knew that sex between the two of them was completely out of the question. Leona Hatton was more than just an MD. She was a battlefield surgeon par excellence; she was also a charter member of Barrabas's elite group of mercenaries. Physical love would hopelessly complicate a relationship like theirs. Such complications could endanger their lives and the lives of the others on the team. More than once, outnumbered, outflanked, she and Barrabas had fought back-to-back under their black flag. They were comrades in arms first, man and woman second. Simply put, survival was more important than sex.

Lee placed the stethoscope against his back and told him to breathe deeply. He did as she asked. From then on, the exam proceeded quickly. In fifteen minutes, Dr. Hatton was through the regimen. Once. Before she put away her instruments, she insisted that he sit still while she reexamined his torso. There was nothing wrong with his muscular development. His chest, arms, shoulders and back were laden with ropy, corded flesh. She ran her fingertips over the cap of his right shoulder. "So much scar tissue," she said, shaking her head.

"Souvenirs of the world's cesspits."

"Relax a minute," she said. She took hold of his arms, each in turn, bending them at the elbows, then straightening them out and rotating them in their sockets.

"How much movement do you figure I've lost?" he said.

"Hard to say. Twenty, twenty-five percent. It's all the scarring and muscle damage."

"Got to practice ducking, huh?" he said.

"No jokes."

"Sure. Let me have it, Doc. What's the prognosis?"

Lee laid her hand gently on the side of his neck. "For a forty-year-old guy who has been shot, stabbed, fragged and tortured by experts, you're in great shape. Heart. Lungs. All okay. Do you ever get numbness in your fingers on the side that had the shattered shoulder?"

"No," he lied, then thought better of it. "Not in the one that counts, anyway." He waggled his trigger finger for her.

The doctor was not amused.

"Bottom line?" he said.

Lee shrugged. "You'll last another year, if you lay off the booze."

Barrabas laughed as he pulled his clothes back on.

"What's so damned funny about a year to live?"

"I never plan that far ahead."

As the doctor opened her mouth to reply, the steady background noise of sea and wind was broken by the howl of a car red-lined in low gear. It was roaring up the rutted track through the field of gorse toward the cottage. Barrabas rose catlike from the sofa and headed for the window.

"Expecting company?" Lee asked.

"There's a Sterling SMG in the cupboard over the sink," he said, flipping up the lid of a crude wooden chest that served as a window seat. "Watch the rear." From the chest he pulled an L1A1 assault rifle, the British version of the FN FAL. He put his back to the stone wall, watching from a safe angle as the small, obviously overloaded car labored up the grade. From behind him the Sterling clacked once; Lee had chambered a live round. They were as ready as they were going to get.

The little car stopped forty feet from the front of the house. The driver's door opened. A huge fat leg appeared. Then an arm and shoulder, equally porcine. The car rocked violently, suspension squeaking as the driver extricated himself from behind the steering wheel. His face was flushed and he was breathing hard as he slowly lumbered up the track to the cottage.

"All clear on the backside," Lee said. "Who is it?"

"The fattest sneaky pete you ever saw."

"Jessup?"

"None other," he said, unbolting the door. "I think we're about to come out of retirement, Doc."

4

In Nate Beck's belly, a half dozen beef-and-potato knishes sat like ten pounds of scrap lead. He dabbed at the clammy moisture that had broken out on his forehead with a cloth napkin.

"Take some more kasha," insisted the little gray-haired lady sitting across the table from him. Using a serving spoon the size of New Jersey, she flopped a monstrous portion of buckwheat groats onto his plate.

Beck could only stare at it, bug-eyed, while the interrogation continued apace.

"Where did you learn this eating like a bird? Your ganef friends? Is this pick, pick, pick how they sit down to eat in those foreign places? Or is it you just don't like your mother's cooking anymore?"

She had only set one place at the table. His. There was enough food laid out for small-town Red Cross disaster relief.

"Ma, I'm stuffed."

She gave him the hurt look, half angry, half sad; it never failed to cut him to the quick. God, how he had missed that ridiculous martyred expression of hers during his forced twenty-month absence.

"Wrap it up for me, Ma, and I'll take it with me when I go."

"You just got here and you're going already?" She threw up her hands in shock and disbelief. "Go, then. Go on, do as you like. Kill me."

"Ma, I'm not going yet."

"Thank the Lord," she breathed.

Beck rose slowly from the table and helped her transfer the food and dishes to the kitchen. She had anticipated leftovers. Set out on the tiled kitchen counter was a double row of large plastic tubs that had once held salt-free, cholesterol-free margarine. As she proceeded to pack each tub with food, she told him, "I want you should keep these containers. They come in handy for a person alone."

For a person on the run from the FBI, they were somewhat less handy, but Nate Beck and his mother did not discuss his criminal past. Or fugitive present. She was aware that he had made the Ten Most Wanted List; he was a celebrity in the Brooklyn neighborhood where he had grown up and where she still lived. It had been a bad week for hardened criminals—that was the only reason he had made it to Number Ten. His crime was succumbing to boredom. Boredom with his wife, Beverly, who liked sex doggie-style: first she would make him sit up and beg for it, then she would roll over and play dead. Boredom with his own easy success in computer design and manufacture. The idea of turning his genius-level IQ to crime started out as a fantasy, then a game, and then he had hit the return key, transferring a million dollars via computer-telephone link to secret bank accounts.

His mother started the wash water running in the sink. Beck looked down at the top of her head. He remembered when he had looked up at her chin. It brought a catch in his throat.

"So tell me," she said, "what are you going to do with your life?"

It was the inevitable question. The one that made guilt ooze from his every pore. It implied, of course, that everything he had done up until that very moment had been a complete and utter waste of time. It was a question that had no answer. Not even "I'm going to find a cure for cancer" would suffice. As sure as heartburn and gas follow knish, the maternal parry to that response would be "A cure for cancer, fine, and what else?"

The truth was, Nathan Beck was happy for the first time in his thirty-three years of life. He was a soldier of fortune. Part of a team of genuine heroes, the SOBs. Like his movie idols, John Wayne and Errol Flynn, Beck and the SOBs were called on to right grievous wrongs, to rescue the innocent, to do the undoable. His joy was something he could not share with his mother because it involved the three horrors of her life: playing with guns, bathing fewer than twelve times a week and travel. If he had told her he was about to go to Afghanistan on a secret mission, she would have dropped dead at the sink.

She began to wash the dishes and he dried. "Your Uncle Hyman is having another cyst removed," she said.

Beck feigned interest, trying to remember who the hell his Uncle Hyman was. Out the kitchen window, he had a view of the side of the brownstone across the alley. A man sat out on the fire escape landing. He had on a T-shirt and jeans and held something to his ear. A transistor radio?

"So how long has it been since you've talked to Beverly?"

Beverly, he remembered. "She divorced me, Ma." She had also turned him in to the Feds for computer theft.

"So you don't still have a mouth? Such a beautiful girl."

Beautiful flanks, Beck recalled. But flanks do not a marriage make. "We're not going to get back together, Ma."

"How do you know if you won't give it a try?"

"I know it wouldn't work."

"You know, you know. You're such a genius, but you're not as smart as you think."

Beck had a sudden sinking feeling in the pit of his stomach. It wasn't the knishes, either. "Ma, you didn't . . ."

She beamed up at him. "It was for your own good. After you told me you were stopping by I called her and we talked, woman to woman. Such a head on her shoulders!"

"You didn't . . ."

"She said she wanted very much to see you again. She promised she would come over for a visit this afternoon."

The guy on the fire escape put the transistor radio to his mouth and talked into it.

Transistor radio, my ass, Beck thought. He grabbed his mother by the shoulders and planted a big juicy kiss right between her eyes. "I love you, Ma. Got to run," he said, doing just that. He could hear her calling his name as he dashed through the living room.

Thanks to his bitch of an ex-wife the Feds had the place surrounded. His mathematical mind whirred in an adrenaline-induced frenzy. Surrounding an apartment house was not the same as trapping a man. He had lived in the building from birth to age twenty, when he got his Master's of Science from Columbia. He knew it better than any FBI man. It was just a matter of making the right move at the right time. Like a game of chess. Beck was very good at chess.

Instead of going out a window onto the fire escape, which he knew the Feds would have covered, instead of trying the hallway outside the apartment's front door, which would also be sealed off, he ducked into his old bedroom.

"Wait, Nathan!" his mother yelled from the living room as he opened the door of the Nate Beck Memorial Closet.

His clothes from high school still hung there. And they were pressed! On the side shelf sat a warped tennis racket and a temple camp backgammon trophy he had won when he was twelve. He kicked aside the shoe rack at the rear of the closet. There was a crack in the seam between two sheets of plasterbroard that made up the back wall. He could see light through it. It was a crack he knew well. As a boy, more than once he had peered through it. That was right after Mrs. Piroshki, the lady next door, had gotten her divorce and was busy entertaining male friends of her former husband in her apartment at all hours of the night and day. Nate had never been able to see much, as the Beck and Piroshki closets were back-to-back and most of the time the Piroshki closet door was closed, blocking the view to the bedroom, but the noises he heard were more than enough to fire his amorous imagination.

Things had changed in the Piroshki household. What he heard now as he peered through the crack was a daytime TV game show.

Beck front snap-kicked the plasterboard. With a solid crunch his foot smashed through past the ankle. Jerking his foot out, he ripped a wider hole in the drywall with his hands. The Piroshki closet door was open. He could see a satin coverlet on the Louis Quinze bed but nothing more. He dived through the opening, lunged across the adjoining closet and burst into the neighbor-lady's bedroom.

"Stop or I'll shoot!" squealed Mrs. Piroshki from under the quilted covers. Only her fat toes, nails painted pearlescent pink, could be seen peeking out at the bottom edge of the coverlet.

"It's all right, Mrs. P.," he said, sprinting past. "It's only Nathan Beck, the arch criminal."

As he ducked into the Piroshki bathroom, he heard one last cry from his mother. Faint, muffled, it came from the hole in the closet wall he had made. "Nathan, don't forget to take your leftovers!"

Beck threw back the shower curtain, scattering to the wind the row of enormous cotton panties hanging from the rod. He opened the bathroom window above the shower stall and, standing on the shower rail, climbed out onto the narrow ledge.

It was three stories down and another two up to the roof. Waves of vertigo swept over him. Only through a supreme effort of will did he fight down the panic reaction. He could see the federal agents starting to move in, blocking off the street with their unmarked cars, running in pairs down the alley, guns drawn. He had gotten out just in time. He turned and grabbed hold of the iron standpipe that ran up to the roof and started to climb, using the evenly spaced pipe brackets for hand- and footholds.

When he reached the roof he was weak in the knees and his heart was pounding. There was no one around. He took a couple of deep slow breaths, then hurried over to the little brick hut that was the entryway to the roof. He found a bent nail on the tarpaper and slipped it through the hasp and ring on the hut's metal door.

So far so good.

Beck loped over to the edge of the building. Eight feet away, across an alley, was the roof of a neighboring brownstone. The distance between the two roofs had been known as "the gap" when he was a boy. The other kids in the neighborhood had always been able to jump the gap. Nate had always been afraid to try because of his vertigo. He was much bigger now, but he was still a card-carrying neurotic. Behind him the hut's metal door rattled against the barred hasp. Then it thudded as someone applied a brawny shoulder to its inside surface.

Beck did not want to go to jail. He was even more afraid of enclosed places than he was of heights. He ran back twenty feet, took a breath and dashed for the edge of the roof. He leaped into space, arms flailing for distance. He landed on his heels on the upraised lip of the opposite roof, did a little more flailing to keep from losing his balance and falling backward into the alley seventy-five feet below. Then he caught himself with a hand and hopped to safety.

As he crossed the roof and started to descend the fire escape on the other side, he laughed aloud at his luck. One more knish and he would have been a goner.

WITH THUMB AND FOREFINGER, Liam O'Toole raised his double shot glass of Bushmill's, holding it up between his face and the Greenwich Village bar's blaring color TV. He rotated the glass as he gazed into it, making red and blue lights dance in its amber depths. For him the Irish whiskey had lost its magical power. The familiar burning warmth from lips to throat to belly no longer freed his poet's soul, no longer electrified his spirit with vibrant bursts of mental imagery, no longer made complex rhymes trip lightly off his tongue.

The stocky, red-haired, ex-U.S. Army captain hadn't come up with an idea for a new verse in weeks, no matter how loaded he had managed to get. All he had accomplished was getting himself eighty-sixed from half the bars in Manhattan. Tonight, on the eve of another desperate mission with Barrabas and the SOBs, even thoughts of his own mortality could not shift the weight of his writer's block.

With a practiced flip of the wrist, O'Toole tossed down the double and slapped the bar for a refill. He wasn't drunk yet, but he was working at it steadily.

Behind him at the row of booths, a couple of miniskirted bimbos were trying to hustle an out-of-towner out of his next mortgage payment. In strident Bronx accents, they cataloged their repertoires of sin, both solo and sister act.

Liam watched as the barman poured him another Bushmill's. No words were exchanged, only money. The bartender took away a ten and brought back lots of ones. O'Toole held up his glass again and squinted into it. The cause of his blockage was no mystery. He hadn't been able to write anything since his experiment with self-publishing had turned to disaster. He had made the leap, gotten his poetry into print all right, but only to discover that no bookstore in New York City would stock him. He had ended up giving all the copies away.

After getting the bum's rush by every publisher, agent and retailer in Manhattan, even the indomitable O'Toole was discouraged.

The bar's padded red vinyl, brass-tack-studded front door swung open and a new customer entered. O'Toole gritted his teeth. He couldn't stand guys who wore designer jeans. What the hell kind of a Renaissance man walked around with a faggot's name stitched across his buns? These particular designer jeans had another count against them: they had ironed-in, knife-edge creases. Counts Three through Five: their owner-occupier had a hairdo like an enraged blond hedgehog, a gray silk shirt with shoulder pads a yard across and an insurance salesman's attaché case.

Sensing richer pastures, the two bimbos immediately deserted their cornered, whimpering prey. The newcomer smiled artificially at the posturing, sleeve-tugging tarts, then leaned over the bar and said, "Is there a guy named O'Toole here?"

The bartender shrugged and continued polishing his beer glass.

"My name's Bash. I write for *Rolling Stone*." He produced a business card, which the bartender pointedly did not look at. "I want to interview this guy O'Toole, and his landlady said he hung out in here."

Liam sized the guy up. Ten-inch biceps. Six-inch wrists. A lightweight. Unless he had a piece in the briefcase, he was no threat. His curiosity roused, O'Toole raised a hand. "Down here," he said.

"Are you Liam O'Toole?"

"Maybe. What sort of interview?"

"For *Rolling Stone*. I want to do an article about his lyrics."

Liam gave the guy a sour look. "Lyrics? He's a poet, not a friggin' songwriter."

"Are you him, then?"

There didn't seem to be any point in denying it. "Yeah."

"And you don't think of yourself as a songwriter?"

"It never crossed my mind," he answered truthfully.

"Don't you watch MTV?"

"Only through a shot glass."

"You really don't know, do you? This is fantastic! Hey, man, your song is number one on the Video Countdown for the fourth week in a row."

Liam sipped his whiskey while the hedgehog rummaged around in his briefcase for tape recorder and notepad.

"Bartender, does that thing get MTV?" the reporter asked.

The bartender nodded.

"Turn it on, please."

As the barman changed channels, the reporter checked his wristwatch. "It should be on any minute now. They've been playing it once an hour like clockwork."

O'Toole had run up against a lot of weirdos in NYC. He made a habit of never letting them interfere with the business of his life. "Another Bushmill's," he told the bartender.

On the tube, a seated duplicate of the hedgehog, only with black hair, breasts and a different shade of lipstick, bared her teeth and said, "Now it's time for number one. Larva Regina and their astounding 'Maggot Picnic.' "

Liam scowled. The title of his self-published book of poetry was *Maggot Picnic*, as was the first poem in the volume. He put down his shot glass and paid attention.

Over a driving, jerky beat, images of the media's war in Vietnam flashed at mind-numbing speed. Jets strafing. Jungle burning in sheets of napalm flame. Naked children running, stick arms over their heads. Bodies in uniform strewn across a dirt road. From a towering long shot of dense tropical rain forest the camera zoomed in on a small clearing. First it was a dot of red amid the green, then it filled the screen. A puddle of red mud. Like a bayonet slash, the first screaming, straining notes of lead guitar cut through the rhythmic background, entering the wall of sound at the same instant the camera caught the four faces of the band. Faces were all that showed, like death masks set out on the surface of the mud. Only the first four inches of their respective dyed fluorescent mohawks were visible.

The singing began, "Red muck-smeared faces, upturned, disembodied, lay gaping on a sanguine, stagnant quicksand sea." The lips of the death masks moved, singing in thunderous unison. The words were O'Toole's. "Islands of paradise for blueback beetles; maternity wards for hairy-legged flies." Computer-enhanced photography made the camera appear to be mounted in the head of one of the aforementioned insects; it seemed to fly right up the nostril of one of the singers.

Everything went red. Then exploded white to a Club Med set. Pretty, tanned, well-oiled girls in string bikinis lounged around a tropical pool on deck chairs, and under gay umbrellas behind them, men in iridescent beetle helmets and three-piece suits briskly exchanged letters of credit. The camera panned to the edge of the pool. Thanks to a deft bit of superimposition, instead of blue water, it contained thousands of squirming six-foot-long maggots.

Four of the maggots had human faces. And mohawks. As Larva Regina began to sing again, this time in an artificial, sped-up falsetto like "Alvin and the Chipmunks," Liam gulped his whiskey and got off the bar stool. He headed for the front exit.

"Hey, you're going to miss the best part," the hedgehog cried. "They drag out this guillotine..."

O'Toole hit the door, then the street.

The reporter pursued him. "I want to talk to you about your poetry, what it means. This could be your big break. A feature story in a national magazine could get you publishing contracts. Movie deals, TV work."

"Fuck off."

"Goddamit, you wait!" the hedgehog said, slapping his hand on Liam's thick shoulder.

It was a big mistake.

O'Toole turned, lifted the reporter and slammed him back against the brick wall, driving the edge of a meaty forearm across the front of his throat. He spoke through gritted teeth an inch from the tip of the man's nose. "You may be Miss Destiny to some soft-bellied, Day-Glo poser but to me you're shit. You got nothing I want. Nothing, understand?"

The hedgehog nodded as best he could. He started to speak, but O'Toole leaned against his larynx, squeezing off his words. And his air.

"If you ever see me again," Liam told him, "run." The moment he relaxed his grip, the reporter twisted away, scrambling, high-kicking down the street. O'Toole watched him disappear around a corner. The sight of a hedgehog in flight made the ex-Army captain feel both buoyant and renewed.

Perhaps because he had spit in the face of impending fame? Or perhaps it was simply a chemical reaction, the exertion of the brief struggle liberating all the booze in his veins?

As he continued down the street, to his surprise a snippet of verse popped into his head. Like a flashbulb firing. Then another. And another. A poem, complete and perfect, appeared before his mind's eye.

Liam paused and in a rumbling, melodious baritone tested his new creation on the captive audience—a lamppost and overflowing dumpster.

5

"I'm gonna show you how it's done, Carla," the rangy pilgrim promised as he dug deep into the bowels of his gargantuan tackle box. He wore cut-off jeans, a tank top that had "Judas Priest" air-brushed across the front and flipflops. His eyes gleamed with excitement as he tied on a new hook and twisted a fresh rubber core sinker onto his line. "Yessir, James 'Bud' Wangis is gonna sorely rip 'em up!"

Carla, a perky, freckled California blonde in an overflowing red halter top and sprayed-on white short shorts, couldn't even fake looking interested in what her date did anymore. She pulled her sun-glasses down off the top of her head and hid behind dark lenses.

"You see, honey, you got to have your..." James Bud's voice trailed off. Carla was staring at the tall, bare-chested Indian sitting cross-legged and silent on the engine cowling among the stacked gear of fifty other ocean anglers.

"Why aren't you fishin', man?" he asked the Indian.

Billy Two, a.k.a. William Starfoot II, regarded James Bud Wangis critically, taking note of the squashed anchovy clinging to his left sideburn and the tiny scales that flecked his chin stubble. The brim of Bud's Padres baseball cap was festooned with a large splotch of gray-white excrement from the sea gulls wheeling frantically overhead.

"I *am* fishin'," the half Osage, half Navaho said flatly.

Wangis grinned and nudged his girlfriend. "Hey, I don't care what you think you're doing, pal. If you don't have a line in the water, you ain't fishin'." He then plucked a live anchovy from the small wells rimming the huge bait tank and pinned it on his hook. "Come on, Carla," he said, waving to her. "Watch me catch a toad."

The blonde smiled and nodded and stayed right where she was.

James Bud didn't notice. He rushed headlong into the melee in progress along the stern rail of the San Diego party boat, *Sundowner*. Some sixty miles off the coast, the eighty-foot sport fisher was drifting alone, surrounded as far as the eye could see by a patch of dark, riffled water, a vast shoal of feeding albacore tuna. Fish in the thirty-pound class were jumping all around the boat. Everyone along the stern was mouth-breathing.

Billy Two watched Wangis rear back and cast over the top of his tightly bunched fellow anglers. Immediately he was swept up in the massive tangle of lines that crisscrossed the stern. If there were fifty fishermen on board, at that moment at least forty-five of them were intimately and unwillingly connected. A spiderweb of monofilament encircled rods, reels, arms, legs, necks. The boat's deckhands, underpaid and overworked, fought desperately with their sidecutters to clear loose lines from lines connected to running fish.

But there was no way to control fishermen who had paid one hundred dollars U.S. apiece for the trip and who now scented blood. The sharp pow of parted fishing lines and departing fish was accompanied by the foulest of oaths, threats of violence and an occasional elbow in the face.

"Gaff! Hey, gaff here!" a voice from the other side of the boat called. A guy yelling for help looked like the male lead in an Italian Hercules film. His rod was bent almost tip to butt and the thirty-pound tuna he was connected to was skittering around on the surface in tight frantic circles. Alex "The Greek" Nanos, a broad grin plastered across his deeply tanned face, was about to land yet another albacore.

One of the deckhands stuck the fish with the gaff and hauled it aboard. It thumped its tail wildly on the deck, splattering its own gore over the legs of bystanders.

"I don't fuckin' believe it!" James Bud exclaimed to no one in particular. "That's the eighth fish he's caught!"

"No, it's the ninth," the deckhand said as he stuffed the still-quivering tuna into one of four already bulging gunnysacks. "And he's the only one with any fish in the bag. You guys ought to watch what he's doing and take some lessons."

"It's all in the way you hold your sphincter," Nanos confided to James Bud. The Greek winked at Bud's girlfriend. And not for the first time, either. "You've got to tense your glutes and sort of—"

"Can I buy one off you?" Wangis interrupted, reaching for his wallet.

"Buy what?"

"One of those sphincters. Same color and hook size you're using."

"Sorry I only brought the one," Nanos said with a straight face. "Never thought I'd have a use for two."

Carla giggled into her hand.

"Time to go back to work," Nanos said. As he did so, he looked over at Billy Two.

The Indian nodded and closed his eyes. He was fishing, all right, fishing with his spirit-mind. He could see the long-finned tuna gliding under the surface of the blue water like enormous swallows. He could sense when they were going to charge under the boat to strike the ball of live bait hiding in the shadow of the hull. He opened his eyes and nodded again to Nanos, who had impaled another anchovy on his hook and stood in the downwind, upcurrent of the stern. The Greek didn't cast—he dropped his bait straight down. And had another hook-up. His reel smoked as the fish took line against a tight drag.

Billy Two conjured up a hungry blue shark and sent it after Nanos's fish. The hooked tuna swam for the bow, away from the phantom predator, away from the tangles.

There was a moan from the rail to the redman's left. He looked over and saw a little boy getting seriously seasick. The ocean was as flat as a mirror. Billy Two patted the kid on the back, told him to wipe his mouth, then said, ''You wanna not be sick? Pull up your shirt.''

The kid wanted more than anything not to be sick. He did as he was told. Billy Two put his thumb on the kid's navel and his middle finger at the tip of his sternum. ''Know what acupressure is? No? Well, it doesn't matter. There's a place right here.'' He pressed with his index finger on a point halfway between navel and sternum. ''If you just hold your own finger right there, right where I'm showing you, and in a couple of minutes you'll be okay.''

The kid sat down beside the huge Indian, finger to abdomen. Gradually the boy lost his ghostly pallor and his breathing became normal again.

"Gaff! Hey, gaff!" Nanos shouted.

James Bud stormed away from the stern rail trailing twenty feet of curlicued monofilament from his right foot. Once again he was out of commission. He glared at the boat's sole "lucky" angler as he threw open the lid of his tackle box.

When the fish was brought aboard, the Greek yawned and stretched, his weightlifter's muscles bulging, gleaming with suntan oil and sweat. "I'm tired of catching fish," he told Billy, handing him the rod. Alex caught Carla's eye, yawned again and announced, "Think I'll go below for a little nap."

Nanos slipped past Billy, climbing down the steep companionway to the tiers of bunks below decks.

"Nothin' I hate worse than a showboat," James Bud said, tying on another hook and sinker. Carla smiled weakly. When her date charged back to the rail, she glanced over her shoulder at the entrance to the bunks.

The kid, meanwhile, seemed to have recovered. "You want to catch a fish?" Billy asked him. The boy's eyes lit up. "Here, take this rod, get bait on and stand over in the corner there. When I tell you, drop the bait in. Got it?"

The boy nodded.

Billy let himself become one with the sea, blanking out everything but the blueness, the coolness. He felt the tuna as they circled, then attacked the bait ball. He opened his eyes and pointed to the boy. His reel sang.

It was a big one. It bent the rod in such a deep curve that the kid could hardly get it off the rail. The boy's eyes were huge with delight. Then the fish took him along the port side up to the bow. A deckhand followed, ready to help out if the need arose.

A whiff of sweet perfume broke Billy's concentration. Out of the corner of his eye he saw slim, tawny thighs and a round bottom in white shorts slip by him. Carla must have felt like a nap, too.

Ten minutes later the deckhand came back dragging a huge albacore by the tail. The boy followed proudly.

"Jackpot fish, for sure," the deckhand said.

James Bud turned back from his tangle, looked at tuna and boy and cursed them both to hell.

"Thanks, mister," the kid told Billy as he returned the rod.

"You don't want to catch another one?" the Indian asked.

"Gee, sure."

"Then, go on—do like you did before. I'll tell you when." Billy shut his eyes. He was just tuning in on the fish when a hand roughly jabbed him.

"Hey, hey, wake up," James Bud said. "You seen Carla? Where'd she go to?"

Billy Two was about to deny everything when, from behind him, from the entrance to the bunk level, a sound erupted. A high-pitched, moaning sound. Obviously feminine, it had a strange rhythmic throb to it.

"Is she down there?"

"She's seasick," Billy said.

"Better go down and see if I can do anything for her."

The Indian caught James Bud by the tank top. "No, you don't want to do that," he said.

"Why not?"

"The poor girl is sick as a dog. Listen to her."

Wangis cocked an ear to the moaning and frowned.

"Trust me, there's nothing you can do for her, except leave her alone. She just wants to die. If you go down there now you're only going to make matters worse."

James Bud glanced back anxiously at the stern rail, at the jumping fish in the water beyond. "Yeah, I guess you're right. Poor thing. Nothing I can do." Wangis rehooked, resinkered, rebaited and recast.

Billy Two waited until James' Bud had retangled, then ducked part of the way down the stairs and peered into the bunk level. The moans were much louder now. And they were in harmony. There was no sign of either the Greek or Carla but on a bunk halfway down the tier a blanket covered a suspiciously large lump. The lump was moving up and down ferociously.

BACK AT THE DOCK THAT EVENING, a surly crowd of anglers departed *Sundowner*. None surlier than James Bud Wangis.

"How'd you do?" a camera-laden tourist type asked as he lugged his gear up from the boat.

"Twenty-five fish for fifty anglers," he said.

"Half a fish per rod. Not too good."

"Yeah," Wangis said. "Especially when two guys caught all twenty-five." He jerked his head back at Nanos and the kid. Billy was helping them push their overloaded fish cart up the dock.

A stocky, red-haired guy in a gaudy aloha shirt stepped in their path. "Wanna sell some fish?" he asked.

"O'Toole!" Nanos exclaimed. "What's happening?"

Liam patted an envelope in his shirt pocket. "Airline tickets," he said. "We got a little job to do. The flight leaves in an hour."

"Do we have time to get cleaned up and changed?" Nanos asked.

O'Toole looked them up and down. Their skin and hair were covered with fish scales and smelled of sea salt, their clothes smeared with sun-dried blood and guts. They smelled like the sea lion enclosure at the zoo. "Not necessary," he told them. "You'll fit right in where we're going."

Nanos and Billy exchanged unpleasant looks. "And just where is that?" the Indian said.

"Pakistan."

6

In the flickering torchlight of the mujahedeen cave, a man lay stretched out on a blanket on the hard ground. His hands and feet were securely bound. Tajik Bula sat some way off, hidden in the deep shadow of a recess in the cave wall. He watched mesmerized as the slowly dying man quivered and shook uncontrollably against the restraints. His head snapped back and forth on his tension-corded neck, his heels drummed the earth. There was no intelligence behind his bulging glassy eyes, only madness and pain. The mujahedeen had stuffed a rag in his mouth so they could get some sleep.

The mistake the man on the ground had made was going back to the gassed village to search for loved ones after the Soviets had left. Even though the yellow fog had dissipated by then, its deadly effects still lingered. The man had only gotten within a mile of the square before being overcome. If he had a wish now, in the melted ruin of his brain, it was for death.

Tajik's black gun stood propped against the cave wall beside him. He could not look at it, could not touch it without feeling sick, desperate, doomed. And he had to hide his feelings of terror. Righteous, true warriors of Islam dozed all around him, their heads toward Mecca. There was no one he could confide in, no one he could confess to. No one but Allah, whom he had betrayed.

The boy buried his face in his sleeves and quietly sobbed. Tajik had thought he could trick the Soviet donkeys, get what he wanted from them without paying a price. His foolishness had cost the lives of every man, woman and child in his village. If the mujahedeen discovered his treachery, there would be no mercy.

The black gun was the cause of it all.

While in Kabul with his uncle, he had met an older teenager in the bazaar. Tajik had been impressed by the boy's clothes, wristwatch and spending money. It was clear now that the older boy had been impressed by Tajik's stupidity. The clothes and watch and money, it turned out, were part of the pay for an agent of Khad. After a couple of days of cementing their friendship with gifts of food and small presents, the agent had revealed himself to Tajik. He asked for information on mujahedeen activity in his area.

Tajik had not been shocked by the disclosure. He had suspected from the beginning that the other boy was working for the government. It was a common practice for the secret police to recruit otherwise unemployable teenagers as information gatherers. When the request finally came, Tajik was ready. He had his tale of lies well rehearsed, and he knew exactly what he wanted in return for it.

In his usual fashion, Tajik had wildly exaggerated the extent of the local farmers' aid to guerrillas. He had made it seem as if they were feeding thousands of rebels. He had wanted to impress the Khad agent and make himself seem more important. Tajik had seen no harm in the deception. At worst he figured the Russians would try to bomb the valley again. Unless they massed a major air strike, it would have a little effect, as before. He knew that there was no way the Soviets would send ground troops into an area that was largely controlled by rebels. He had received a solemn promise from the agent that his own family would be unharmed. He had even drawn the older boy a map of the village with his house clearly marked. There had never been any mention of an impending gas attach.

What he had done, he had done for the black gun. For status. He had wanted to be a hero without taking any risks. A lazy boy's fantasy had turned into a nightmare.

He could not give back the gun.

He could not bring back his family.

He could not bring back the village.

He had destroyed his past and his future with a few thoughtless words. All that Tajik had left was his own life. And that, too, was in mortal jeopardy—if his betrayal was found out by the rebels and if it wasn't. It was a cruel twist of fate that the boy who'd played hero now had to act like one. He was a mujahedeen. He had to go into battle, his black gun against Soviet tanks and heavy artillery. He had to follow the orders of hardened warriors who were not afraid to die, indeed, who wanted nothing more than to die in the service of Allah, to further the cause of His jihad, holy war.

From where he sat, Tajik could see his friend Aziz sleeping on the cave floor with the others. He was curled on his side. Next to him was the ancient Lee-Enfield bolt-action rifle he had been issued. The weapon's barrel was rusted, its stock chipped and cracked. In his hand Aziz clutched a pitiful 8-round cache of .303-caliber bullets. Tears again flooded Tajik's eyes. Aziz was everything he wasn't. He had the courage and strength of will to be a warrior. He deserved to be in this place, with these people. It was so terribly unfair.

Tajik slumped back in his niche in the wall and eventually cried himself to sleep.

7

Barrabas strode through the Kachaghari refugee camp on the edge of Peshawar, Pakistan, one hundred miles east of Kabul. From the glassless windows, doorless doorways of mud and straw hovels, from the parted flaps of government surplus tents, he drew stares from old and young. He could see the fear and dread in their eyes; it made his stomach coil tight. They had been driven from their homes, forced to walk away from everything they could not carry. They left behind villages "rubblized" by Soviet saturation bombing, livestock slaughtered by machine gun, fields and wells poisoned. Anything that could help support or supply the guerrilla movement had been destroyed.

Pakistan had, after the way of Islam, opened its borders to the victims of Russian terror. Now there were three million of them in similar camps all along the frontier. Too many for the country to absorb, too many to deal with. For the newcomers there was a four-month wait for ration cards. For the old-timers, those who had been in camp long enough to have constructed "temporary" shelters out of native straw and brown clay, there was no certainty, no guarantee that this morning or tomorrow they might be without the meager protection of the reeking, unsanitary camp.

Even with his head of shocking white hair covered by the hood of his M-65 field jacket, Barrabas could not pass for one of them. He was too big, and his skin, though tanned, was several shades too light. In occupied Kabul, he would have been pegged as a Russian and, if caught walking alone, been summarily disemboweled and left in the gutter to die.

Barrabas was not walking alone through the refugee camp. The blond man matching him stride for stride was even bigger and broader than he was.

Gunther Dykstra wrinkled his nose at the pervasive stench of open latrine and cursed at length.

"Something wrong?" Barrabas asked.

"Colonel, when the wind blows wrong in this dump you'd swear you'd been hit by a truck."

"Look on the bright side, Gunther. We've spent our last night in Kachaghari. You're never going to have to smell this place again."

"That's great, Colonel, but do you think we could walk a little faster? I'm about to lose my breakfast."

Barrabas picked up the pace. He knew it wasn't just the aroma of the camp that was bothering Dykstra. Gunther had survived much worse accommodations in southeast Asia. For the past forty-eight hours they had both been eating local food, the Dutchman rather more carelessly than his American friend. As a result, Gunther had acquired a mild case of "Pakistan tummy." It wasn't his first bout with it; it wouldn't be his last. It was an occupational hazard of his.

Dykstra, along with his sister, Erika, owned and operated Netherlands Imports Management. Though based in Amsterdam, it did extensive business throughout the Third World. The company had some "legitimate" dealings, but they were merely a cover. The real business of Netherlands Imports was smuggling on an international scale. Gold, works of art, gems, electronics equipment; they handled everything but drugs. Barrabas had first met the Dykstras during the Vietnam war when they were ferrying men and material into Laos and Cambodia for the CIA. Theirs was an enduring friendship, one cemented with blood, with debts of life and honor.

They passed under the walls of the town's old Mogul fortress, with its blue-domed towers, a relic of a long-lost Indian Empire that had once stretched from the Bay of Bengal to the west beyond Kabul. Soon they came to the main street of the Quissa Khawani bazaar. It was paved with asphalt and lined with stalls selling rugs, used books, clothing, vegetables. Strung high overhead, across the street between the opposing buildings, was a tattered, faded ocher banner that proclaimed the eternal glory of God.

"It's this way," Gunther said, leading them down a narrow lane through the gold bazaar called the Street of Small Reward. On either side of them, objects cast, painted, plated in gold were openly displayed.

They continued on, through an even narrower lane to the Murad Market, the refugee bazaar. Most of the stalls were rented by Afghan carpet sellers, silversmiths and antique dealers. Gunther led the way through a small iron-fenced courtyard and what appeared to be a private path alongside a crumbling two-story building. They rounded the corner, facing a bleak, narrow chasm of gritty alley and a solid wood door painted in bright pink enamel.

Gunther paused before he knocked. He could see the concern in Barrabas's angular face. The armaments on this mission were crucial not only to its success but to the SOBs' survival. The ex-Army colonel didn't like putting that power into the hands of a man he had never met. "Hey, relax," Gunther told him. "I've known this guy for years. I trust Abdul Khalis with my life. With my sister's life. He is a keen businessman, but always a straight shooter. And he hates the Commies with a passion that will curl your hair."

"Sounds like my kind of guy," Barrabas said.

Gunther's knock was answered by a short, mahogany-skinned man with a thick black mustache and a large smile. He wore the traditional cream-colored baggy pants, a matching long-sleeved shirt and a yellow sweater vest. All were stained with spots of oil. He had a coarse-spun wool fez on his head and low under his left arm was a leather shoulder holster and a .45-caliber Colt automatic. The single supporting holster strap over his right shoulder was actually a bandolier, three inches wide, for fifty jacketed hollowpoint ACP rounds.

"Ahh, Mr. Gunther," he said, extending a hand adorned with a massive gold ring and a wrist bearing a gold Rolex. "Your six comrades arrived some time ago. I have done my humble best to make them comfortable."

"Abdul Khalis," the Dutchman said, "this is another comrade."

The Afghan's smile broadened. "At last I meet the man with the white hair. I am honored."

"As am I," Barrabas said, shaking the gun dealer's offered hand.

"This way, please," Abdul Khalis said.

Barrabas and Gunther followed him down a dim hallway and into a room with a heavy steel door.

Seated on the floor on rich but grease-spotted red Oriental rugs were the rest of the SOBs. After the local custom, they were all in their stocking feet. They were drinking tea from tiny glasses. Behind them, on wooden racks along the floor, hanging by slings from pegs in the wall were hundreds of wooden-stocked rifles.

"Hey, Colonel," Nanos said, putting his glass down on a silver filigree tray and gesturing around the room, "what do you think of the decor?"

"Looks like a museum."

Most of the weapons displayed were at least forty years old, World War II or before. Bolt-action Model 98 German Mausers, British Lee-Enfields. There were a few more recent bolt-action hunting rifles, with raised cheekpieces on their buttstocks and fancy checkering on pistol grips, and three new Pakistani reproductions of the Thompson Model 1927 SMG, but most were military arms and well worn.

"Okay, Adbul," Gunther said, "show us the good stuff."

The little man rubbed his palms together. "Only the best for you, Mr. Gunther."

He took a ring of keys from a chain around his neck and opened another metal door hidden behind a curtain. He entered the closet and in a moment returned bearing an armload of folding-stock AKs. He placed them reverently on the rug. "These

Kalashnikovs are all in perfect condition. Hardly used at all, except for target practice.''

"You don't mind if we examine them, do you?'' Barrabas asked.

The gun merchant stiffened ever so slightly. "These weapons did not come to me through the black market,'' he assured the colonel in an even voice. "I bought each of them directly from a Soviet Army deserter.''

Gunther broke it. "We are paying top dollar, Abdul,'' he reminded him.

The little man puffed out his chest. "I am confident that you will find the guns as I have described them.'' As the SOBs proceeded to quickly field-strip the AKs, Abdul pulled out his battery-powered minicalculator and began to figure out the cost, less his usual discount. "I will give you the same break on the price I give to the mujahedeen,'' he said. "Twenty percent off list to all killers of Communists.''

Claude Hayes peered down an AK barrel and grinned. "I've seen some clean guns before,'' the black man said, "but the bore on this baby's so bright, it's almost blinding.''

The other SOBs agreed.

"Okay, put them back together,'' Barrabas said.

"We'll take these and another three like them,'' Gunther told the gun dealer after the inspection was complete.

"My pleasure," Abdul said, returning to the closet.

When each mercenary had a serviceable weapon, the merchant said, "How many rounds of ammunition will you be needing?"

"Ten 30-round clips per man," Barrabas told him. "Three hundred rounds each."

"Times eight," Abdul said, tapping on his calculator. "That's twenty-four hundred rounds at two dollars U.S. per round."

"Ouch!" Liam said. The going rate in the States for 7.62x39 millimeter ComBloc ammo was only about thirty-five cents a shot.

"We could also use something that packs a bigger wallop," Gunther said. "For tanks."

Abdul Khalis's eyes lit up. "I have exactly what you want," he said, rushing out of the room. He came back dragging an oblong wooden crate by its rope handle. The marking on the outside of the box was in Arabic and English. The English said: Sewer Pipe.

The little man used a Lee-Enfield bayonet to pry up the lid. Once it was off, he began pulling armloads of excelsior packing from the box's interior and throwing it out on the rug.

The SOBs crowded around to have a look at what he had.

"Those are the shortest lengths of sewer pipe I've ever seen," Nate Beck said.

Indeed, the olive drab tubes were only a shade longer than three feet.

"When did you ever see sewer pipe with carrying handles?" O'Toole said, lifting one of the things from its niche in the box's built-in rack. The tube had large protective pads over both ends.

"LAW 80s," Barrabas said.

Liam removed the pads and turned the weapon over. When he put the LAW on his shoulder the carrying handle became the hand grip for firing. "This beauty replaced the M-72," he said. "It's state of the art. It fires a 94 mm HEAT projectile." He pointed to the front underside of the tube, at a small hole in the end of the grip assembly. "It also has a 9 mm spotting rifle built in. The special 9 mm bullet is ballistically matched to the LAW rocket. Where the bullet hits, the rocket hits." He patted the rifle magazine, horizontal to the grip on the left side of the LAW. "You've got five rifle shots to get the range on your target. You've got one HEAT projectile to do the job."

"We'll take eight," Barrabas said.

Abdul beamed and nodded, poking his calculator. "Will there be anything else?"

Gunther shook his head. "Just the food and medical supplies I already told you about. And the transportation in and out, of course."

Abdul gave his calculator a last poke. "Shall we settle the bill now?" He showed Barrabas the figure in the liquid crystal display panel.

The white-haired man did not flinch. He opened his shirt and took out a thickly packed money belt. From the belt he withdrew banded sheaves of hundred dollar bills. The belt was almost empty when he finished.

Abdul counted every stack twice. Then, satisfied, he dumped the cash into a woven satchel. "I will go get Naazmomad now," he said.

Gunther addressed the others. "His cousin will lead us where we want to go..."

"And get us back?" Nanos said.

"My cousin Naazmomad has made the trip to Kabul dozens of times," Abdul assured him. "He has killed three gunships with nothing but a bolt-action Enfield."

"How many have killed him?" Billy muttered. And got a hard look from the colonel.

As the gun merchant headed for the door he looked at Dr. Hatton and stopped short. He bent down and threw back a cushion, exposing a padlocked metal strongbox. He unlocked the box and took out a gun and holster, which he laid at Lee's bare feet. "With my compliments," Abdul said, grinning fiercely.

Dr. Hatton withdrew the hogleg Smith from its oiled shoulder leather. It was a stainless steel beast-

and-a-half. A Model 629 in .44 Mag with an eight-and-three-eighths-inch barrel and carved ivory grips.

"A woman of your beauty should always have protection close at hand," the Afghan said, lowering his head.

"You are too kind," Lee said, thumbing open the loading gate, half-cocking the hammer and spinning the cylinder.

"What do we get?" Nanos asked.

"We ain't pretty," Billy Two said.

"Speak for yourself," the Greek told him.

After Abdul left the room to fetch their guide, Barrabas called the meeting to order. "Sorry about this last-minute briefing, but this is a rush job and there was no time to arrange a get-together beforehand." He took a folded piece of paper out of his coat pocket and spread it on the rug in front of them. "This is the target," he said, pointing at the five-sided, three-towered enclosure depicted in the sketch. "It's located twenty kilometers north of Kabul. Four hundred years ago it was a stone fort for the Mogul troops. The Soviets refurbished it after the '79 invasion and are using it to garrison 150 men and a BTR-60 armored personnel-carrier unit. It also is a storage area for a new type of chemical warfare material they are testing on the rebels."

"I think I hear my mama calling," Nanos said, half rising from the rug.

Hayes caught him by the belt and jerked him back. "Your mama is too damn late."

"These outer walls are more than six feet thick," Barrabas went on. "They are rocket proof. The three stone towers are armed with heavy machine guns on motorized turrets. Our best intel is that they're all 12.7 mm Kalashnikov tank MGs, two to a tower. There's a narrow catwalk around the top of the wall with open stairs leading down to ground level. The chemical storage bunker is just opposite the helicopter landing pad in the center of the compound. On the right are the barracks, generators and water and diesel storage tanks. On the left is the vehicle repair area and ammo dump."

"What are those little cone-shaped things on the top of the wall?" Hayes asked.

"Kliegs," Barrabas answered. "They light up the interior of the fort as well as the surrounding terrain."

"Well, I see only two ways in," Liam said. "Through the front gate or from the helicopter pad."

"We're going in the front gate," Barrabas said.

"Holy shit," Nanos groaned.

"The plan is to hijack a BTR-60 on patrol and drive it back inside the walls," the colonel continued. "From there we break into the bunker, locate the chemical warheads and rig them to blow up inside the bunker if they are moved. We're not looking for a big bang here. We just want the gas released . . . as if by accident."

"Even if the bunker itself is breached by the explosion," Nate said, "a low-yield blast shouldn't spread the poison too far outside the compound."

"I can see how we get in and do the job," Dr. Lee said. "It's tricky, but not impossible. What I want to know is how the hell are we supposed to get out?"

"Diversion," Barrabas said. "If we crack this big diesel tank, let the fuel spread out over the compound, then set it alight, it should keep the reds busy while we rapel the outer wall and scoot."

"Diversion, hell!" Liam exclaimed. "We're talking roast Commie City."

"How far from here is the target?" Nate asked.

"Measured in miles, about a hundred," Barrabas told him. "Measured in days on pack horse it's going to be four each way, barring the unforeseen."

With a discreet clearing of his throat to announce his return, Abdul Khalis entered the gun room with his cousin in tow. "This is my cousin Naazmomad," he said proudly. "Killer of gunships."

The killer was even shorter than Abdul, barely five foot five in his combat boots. He had a khaki turban wrapped around his head and sported a full mustache like his cousins. He had a heavy growth of black stubble on his face, running up over his cheekbones and down the front of his neck to meet the similar shrubbery sprouting from the open collar of his fatigue shirt.

"Does he speak English?" Gunther asked.

"Oh, yes, he speaks as good as I do," Abdul answered.

Naazmomad nodded and smiled. He had no front upper teeth.

"Is everything ready for us to leave tonight?" Barrabas asked their guide.

Naazmomad nodded. He looked down at the weapons heaped on the rug and again showed his prominent gap.

"He likes our taste," Billy Two said.

The guide knelt and patted one of the LAW 80s. Then he reached into his breast pocket and pulled out a loop of twine on which something that looked like dried figs had been strung.

"No, thanks," Nate said, "not hungry."

Naazmomad shook his head. He pointed to the "figs" and then to his own ears.

"Ugh, I'm really not hungry now," Beck groaned.

The little man wasn't through, though. While his cousin Abdul beamed, Naazmomad raised his arms to shoulder level and, swaying them slightly up and down made a Bronx cheer, propeller sound with his mouth. Then he stopped and held up the necklace of ears, grinning his toothless grin.

"We get the picture," Barrabas told him.

"Hey, I don't know about you guys," Nanos said, looking up from the necklace that Naazmomad had offered for his inspection, "but I feel better already."

8

Gregor Andreyev peered around the front bumper of the 6x6 truck. Ahead, the rest of the fifteen-vehicle convoy was still stopped, the lead vehicle out of sight around a bend in the road. The olive drab trucks and the hillside were tinted with purple evening light. Behind and below them, the out-skirts of Kabul twinkled. They hadn't gotten very far from the garrison before the first breakdown. The lieutenant was nowhere in sight—a good thing since he was hopping mad. Gregor turned back to the 6x6's running board and his friend and fellow private, Yuri Temkin.

"Is it okay?" Yuri asked.

"They'll be at it for another half hour at least," he said, a wild sparkle in his eyes and a leer twist-ing his lips. "Let's blow some smoke."

As he sat down on the running board, Yuri fished around in his fatigue jacket pocket, pulling out a blackened stub of briar pipe, matches and a little painted tin box. He pried open the tin box and carefully took from it a brown chunk the size of a sugar cube.

"Come on, fire it up, fire it up," Gregor said.

Yuri dropped the cube into the bowl of the pipe, stuck the pipe in his mouth and lit a wooden match. He applied the flame to the bowl of the pipe and sucked, vigorously puffing his cheeks in and out.

The pungent aroma of burning hashish rode the faint evening breeze. It made Gregor's mouth water. "Me, me," he said, reaching for the pipe.

Yuri let him have it. The two of them smoked hard and fast, passing the pipe back and forth, coughing violently from the superheated smoke. Finally, Gregor, his nose running, tongue parched, waved off the hash. His head was reeling madly. He had had enough. A warm, sticky feeling spread over his belly and chest and a broad, idiot's grin spread across his face.

"Rock and roll," he said. "We need some hard-beating rock and roll."

Yuri drew a pocket-size cassette tape player from his coat and turned it on, keeping the volume low. Gregor began to sing along at once. "Big girls don't cry," he sang, "they don't cry-eye-eye..."

"Shut up," Yuri told him. "I can't hear the music."

Gregor contented himself with humming along with the great Frankie Valli. He leaned back against the truck door, hugging himself. Afghanistan was a shithole, right enough. Its people were all religious maniacs who delighted in very primitive revenge: disemboweling, castration, flaying alive. The women covered themselves up from head to foot and they wouldn't spread their legs for money. The native food both stank and made one sick. The only good thing about Afghanistan was its smoke. The shithole had some of the finest hashish on the planet. In Gregor's opinion, even that wasn't worth fighting over.

The war in Afghanistan was unfair to everyone. Unfair to the dirt-scratching farmers who made up most of the country's population, but even more unfair to the likes of Gregor Andreyev, who had been dragged from the relative comfort of his native Leningrad, his family, his friends, his vodka, and forced to serve as part of an army of occupation.

"I wish we had a videotape recorder," Yuri said.

"Mmm," Gregor murmured contentedly, trying to imagine the wonderful device, with its remote control, slow motion, stop frame, automatic rewind.

"Think of the films we could watch!" Yuri said, warming to a familiar subject.

"Strangler films!"

"Yes, my friend, strangler and butcher and teenage sorority slaughterhouse. All the very best."

"Just like Americans."

"And we could play back the good parts."

"The shower scenes."

"We could run them over and over."

"Perhaps we should desert, Yuri."

The other private winced. He pushed his back away from the truck door and looked around. He saw no one. "You've got to keep things like that to yourself, Gregor. For all we know there's a GRU man hiding under the front axle."

Gregor, emboldened by the dope, shrugged off his friend's concern. "GRU! Who have they caught recently? Corporal Smerdlenko auctioned off his weapons and boots to the highest bidder in the bazaar in Kabul and just walked away. That was more than two months ago."

"He's probably dead."

"Dead drunk, you mean." Gregor gave Yuri a hard look. "Say, you don't swallow all that stuff the officers feed us about AWOL soldiers being murdered, do you?"

Yuri started putting the hash-smoking gear away.

"That's just a trick to get us so scared we won't desert."

"If we did desert, there'd be no place to run," Yuri said. "We couldn't go back to Russia. We couldn't stay in Kabul. We'd have to join the rebels." A look of disgust passed over his face. "They eat goat shit three times a day."

"If we could get to Pakistan—"

His words were cut off by the sound of boots crunching on the gravel of the road's shoulder. Yuri shut off the tape player and jammed it inside his coat as the two of them stood bolt upright at attention.

"Did I hear music, Private?" the lieutenant demanded. "I hope I didn't hear music."

AZIZ AND TAJIK NEARED the security checkpoint on the only road leading into Kabul from the south. Other foot travelers were queued up, being questioned and pat-searched by uniformed Afghan puppet-government soldiers. Civilian cars and trucks were also stopped in a line, submitting to search.

Both boys were nervous.

With cause.

Aziz had a PG-7 rocket grenade strapped nose-down to the inside of each of his thighs, hidden among the voluminous folds of his loose-fitting trousers. Tajik carried his precious black gun, field-stripped and then some. Not only had he removed the magazine, receiver cover, recoil spring guide and guide rod, bolt carrier assembly and bolt and gas cylinder tube but he had taken off the butt-stock and pistol grip, as well, so he, too, could get the main portion of the assault rifle down one of his pant legs. The Kalashnikov buttstock was taped to his other leg, along with a cloth bag that contained the loose gun parts. Inside the front of his shirt were two loaded AK 30-round clips.

Aziz would have been much more nervous if the line to the checkpoint had been moving faster. Both he and Tajik tended to clank when they walked.

This was to be their first mission with the mujahedeen. They were sneaking weapons and munitions into the Kabul area for use in a night attack against a Soviet convoy.

When they finally reached the soldiers, Tajik was trembling all over. Perspiration poured down the sides of his face. Aziz was afraid the boy might break down and confess on the spot, before the first question was asked. He moved in close behind him and pinched him hard in the back. Tajik turned, his eyes wide at the pain. It calmed him down a little.

The soldier waved them on without even asking where they were going. They didn't pay too close attention to teenagers, especially young teenagers. That was why the rebels used teenagers to ferry supplies and information back and forth across enemy lines.

The boys shuffled slowly along beside the road.

"See?" Aziz said softly after they had gone a little way. "There was nothing to worry about. It was easy."

"Easy for you," Tajik countered. "This gun is heavy and the front sight has worn away the skin on my ankle."

Aziz shut up. To respond was to encourage more whining. He only wished he had Tajik's problem. But his hopes were high that tonight he would capture his own black gun. He had prayed over it much. And if not that, at least he would avenge in part the murder of his family.

A Toyota pickup, its bed overflowing with young people, passed on the road next to them.

"Hey, you!" someone from the pickup shouted at them.

Shouted and pointed.

The two boys did not wait. Aziz took off to the left, Tajik to the right. Aziz made it around the corner of a mud-brick building. Hearing no footfalls behind him, he stopped and looked back to see if he was being pursued. He wasn't. Whoever it was had gone after Tajik.

Aziz quickly backtracked. He found his friend and another boy, older and much bigger, talking heatedly in front of a closed shop. The bigger boy had hold of Tajik's shoulders and kept shoving him back into the corrugated metal shutter over the shop entrance, making his head bang against it.

"Stop that!" Aziz said, running up.

The older boy glowered at him. He had a sharp, hatchet profile and was dressed in expensive Western-style clothes. "Who are you?" he demanded.

Aziz returned the question. "Who are you?"

Tajik answered in a shaky voice. "Aziz, this is my half cousin, Khwaja. I owe him some money from the last time I was here."

Khwaja slammed Tajik against the shutter, making it and his head rattle one last time. "Don't you disappoint me, cousin," he warned. He brushed off the front of his leather sports jacket and sauntered away.

Aziz waited until he was out of sight before he said anything. "How much do you owe him?"

"Too much," Tajik said dejectedly.

This made no sense to Aziz. He could not imagine why Tajik would have borrowed a large sum of money. Nor could he imagine anyone being so stupid as to lend money to a fourteen-year-old boy. Tajik's expression was so distraught that Aziz felt he had to say something positive to cheer him up. "If worse comes to worst," Aziz told him, "you could always sell the black gun to pay back your cousin."

Tajik gave him a strange look.

"We'd better go," Aziz said. "We're still a half an hour from the meeting place."

After forty minutes of circling through the shantytown perimeter of Kabul, the boys arrived at the rendezvous point. It was a narrow unlit stretch of road that wound between the foothills. Someone hissed at them from the bushes on the downslope side of the road and they climbed down the grade to join the others. Aziz removed his trousers, then the PG-7 rockets. Tajik unburdened himself of the dismantled AK, then he and Aziz set about reassembling it in the failing light.

The kill zone was up against the side of a steep hill. The straight bit of road was so narrow that the convoy could not turn around. The plan was to stop the first and last trucks in the line with RPGs, then slaughter the soldiers trapped in the trucks in between. This was not primarily a raid for supplies or ordnance. It was primarily a terror attack.

As darkness fell, Aziz could feel the tension growing among the row of men sitting in the dirt of the hill slope. He could hear their muttered prayers.

"They're not going to come," Tajik whispered to Aziz for the twentieth time. It was a kind of prayer, as well.

Then they heard the sound of heavy trucks laboring up the grade in low gear. The glare of headlights swept around a turn and onto the kill zone straightaway. Shadowy human forms on either side of Aziz began to move, creeping up the slope to a point just below the edge of the road. Aziz and Tajik moved forward along with the others, maintaining their position in the middle of the string.

The trucks looked huge as they lumbered past.

Then came a shouted command from the mujahedeen leader.

Men at either end of the ambush line popped up above the edge of the road. RPGs on their shoulders flared, delivering short squeaks of rocket ignition, and even shorter squeals of flight to the front wheels of the targeted 6x6s. The night was ripped by a pair of almost simultaneous booms and a brilliant flash of light that cast long shadows down the hillside.

The first and last trucks in the convoy coasted to a stop, their hoods up, their cabs on fire. The trucks in between skidded to panic stops.

"Allah e akbar! Allah e akbar!" shouted the soldiers of God as they burst from concealment over the lip of the road.

Aziz and Tajik were swept up and over along with the human wave.

Gunfire, automatic and single shot, erupted all around them. Muzzle-flash and leaping flame lit up the daisy chain of trucks. Bullets whined back at the freedom fighters, cutting holes in the night.

In the flickering light Aziz saw Tajik had frozen beside the roadway. He stood still, firing his black gun from the shoulder.

He fired full-auto.

He had his eyes closed.

"Look out!" Aziz shouted at him.

Too late. One of the other mujahedeen made the mistake of stepping into Tajik's withering but unaimed field of fire. The man's dirty fez and the back of his head flew off. He toppled onto his face, dropping his ancient .303 Short Magazine Lee-Enfield. Aziz waited until Tajik's AK came up empty, a matter of seconds at the rate of fire he was unleashing, then grabbed the fallen rifle. With it raised to hip height, he charged the passenger side of the cab of the nearest truck. As he did so, the door on the other side opened and the passenger and driver ducked out.

Aziz raced around the front of the 6x6 and, seeing only one running man, stopped, aimed quickly and fired. The hard jolt of recoil sent the SMLE's brass buttplate ramming into his shoulder. The running man staggered, struck high in the back. Aziz got the short bolt action cycled in rapid order. His target meanwhile had run head-on into the grille protector of the next truck behind. He bounced off the bumper and hit the ground flat on his back.

Aziz ran up and put the muzzle of the rifle to his forehead.

The soldier begged in Russian to be spared. There was hashish on his breath.

The boy did not shoot. He held the wounded man in place until the shooting around them had stopped and the leader of the rebel band slapped a hand warmly on his shoulder.

"Good work, Aziz," the leader said. Then he called for the others to quickly gather around.

When they had, he said, "Tie this one to the bumper." As the stone-faced mujahedeen obeyed, from the folds of his shirt he drew out a long, thin-bladed knife.

GREGOR ANDREYEV was on a bad trip.

He hung, limpetlike, to the undercarriage of the 6x6, his back wedged against the transmission housing. With his fingers and the toes of his boots he held onto the truck frame's I-beams.

Not twenty feet away, his friend and fellow doper, Yuri Temkin was even more bummed. It was understandable as he was the one being skinned alive. The ingestion of a massive dose of some of the world's finest hashish was doing nothing to dull his agony. The screams that burst from his throat were so piercing and so terrifyingly near that they made Gregor wet himself.

As he hung there, Gregor made a whole string of promises. He promised never to swear again. Never to drink liquor to excess again. Never to smoke dope. Never to fool around with whores. He promised to be a good soldier and model citizen. He wasn't promising all this to the lieutenant or even the party boss back in Leningrad. Gregor Andreyev, an atheist for all his twenty-five years, had finally found God.

Yuri's torture would not end with a single rifle shot. Gregor knew it. The mujahedeen never handed a coup de grace to wounded enemies. If there were no women around to hack off a foe's private parts and feed them to him, he was left belly up in the dirt to face the will of Allah.

Yuri Temkin's shrill cries had dwindled into a steady, soft mewling. The sound was interrupted by breaking glass and a whoosh of sucking air. From the truck in front came a sudden blaze of orange light.

Gregor realized what was happening too late. Before he could make his cramped fingers let go, before he could get himself free of the truck's undercarriage, the crude firebomb shattered on the ground directly underneath him. For an instant he smelled gas, then everything exploded into flame and his flesh began to melt.

For Yuri the fire was an act of redemption; for Gregor it was nothing short of hell.

9

Aziz and Tajik fled the line of burning trucks, backtracking through the fringes of the city. Beyond the security checkpoint, they would bisect the road north. They carried their rifles in their hands as they ran. There was no point in taking the weapons apart for the return trip. As there was a 10:00 P.M. military curfew in Kabul, enforced on penalty of death, they had nothing to lose by having their guns ready.

The lights of the city of two million paled under the hard white glare of Soviet and Afghan Army searchlights that swept the surrounding rocky hills for guerrillas. The guerrillas put on a light show of their own, occasionally launching hit-and-run rocket attacks on enemy hard targets inside Kabul. The orange tracks of rockets, mostly SAM-7s liberated from the Russians, blazed across the night sky, impacting with earthshaking whumps. The Soviets absorbed their own ordnance and returned fire with tank cannon and heavy machine guns.

Howling tracer rounds green-lined the terrain, valley to hill slope.

In Kabul every night was the Fourth of July.

As he ran, Tajik stumbled and fell several times. He also went the wrong way more than once, and Aziz had to call him back. If anything, Tajik seemed more nervous after the mission than he had been before. Aziz thought he understood the reason. The other boy had by his own incompetence and cowardice shot and killed a true mujahedeen. In the dark and confusion of the attack only Aziz had seen what had happened. Irony of ironies, the rebel leader had heartily commended both boys for their bravery. Aziz had said nothing. In truth, he did not know what to say.

When they reached the far side of the city, Tajik stopped against a wall, out of breath. They were at Zarghuna Maidan, "Chicken Street," where the poultry market was held during the day. It was now closed down tight. Tajik said, "Aziz, I have something important to do in this neighborhood. Will you wait for me here? I won't be long."

Against his better judgment Aziz agreed. He watched Tajik slink off into the shadows. It was too dangerous to be in the city alone after curfew. Aziz made up his mind in an instant: he would follow and back up his friend, if necessary.

For his part, Tajik had no idea he was being trailed. He was too preoccupied with his own fear.

He turned down an alley off Chicken Street, found the doorway he was looking for and crept up a steep flight of adobe stairs. He knocked lightly on the door at the top.

"Yes?" said a voice from within.

"It's your half cousin," Tajik said.

Khwaja opened the door and let him in. Though it was not the first time he had been to the older boy's lodgings, he was struck by the variety and quality of the boy's material possessions: color television, radio, stereo, Scandinavian furniture.

The Khad agent did not offer him a seat after he closed the door. With one hand, Khwaja grabbed the muzzle of the AK; with the other he grabbed the younger boy's loose shirt by the throat and twisted it tight enough to choke him.

Tajik let him take the gun.

Khwaja shoved him aside. He removed the AK magazine and tucked it inside his trouser waistband. After he checked to make sure the chamber was clear, he thrust the gun back at the boy. "Here, have it back," he said. "You earned it."

Tajik took the weapon. "Why didn't you tell me the truth before?" he demanded. "Why didn't you tell me what was really going to happen to my village?"

"Would you have helped me if I had?"

"Of course not!"

Khwaja laughed at him. "What do you have to complain about? You got what you wanted. Now you are a mujahedeen, a hero." He paused, then added through a smile, "Now you can be of some real use to me."

Tajik felt his knees begin to shake.

"Come here," the older boy said, gesturing for him to follow to a table on which a map lay spread out. "Pick up that pen and mark the spot where the mujahedeen cave stronghold is."

"They'll kill me."

"If you don't mark the spot, I'll see to it that they find out who betrayed your village."

Tajik knew Khwaja would do it. He started to cry.

The older boy slapped him hard across the face. "Stop that! And do as I say!"

Tajik obeyed as best he could. His hand shook as he picked up the pen and his tears spattered on the map.

"Are you sure that is the location?"

Tajik nodded at the X he had drawn.

"Well, we are going to make double sure," Khwaja told him. He went over to a cupboard, took out a shoebox. From the shoebox he removed a small black plastic box. It had a switch on top, a small red on-off light and a retractable antenna. "This is a radar homing beacon. When you get back to the cave, I want you to find a safe place to hide this outside the entrance. It must be no farther than twenty-five meters from the opening. You simply turn on the switch, the light will go on and you raise the antenna like this."

"What are you going to do?"

"You don't want to know, my little hero. If you do this right for me, I will give you a watch like this." He showed Tajik his gold Rolex. "Or you can have another black gun, if you'd prefer."

Numbed by his own helplessness, Tajik barely felt Khwaja push the box into his hand. After dropping the AK magazine into Tajik's pants pocket, the older boy ushered him quickly back out the door.

On the landing Khwaja told him, "If you do this wrong, you know what will happen." Then the Khad agent stepped back inside his apartment and closed the door, leaving Tajik standing alone on the landing in the dark.

He was not the only one in the dark. Aziz waited at the bottom of the stairs. He had seen Khwaja and had heard only the last cryptic remark. Before his friend could turn and start down, Aziz took off running, back the way he had come.

Nothing made sense to him anymore. His family and village, never a threat to the occupiers, had been wantonly, savagely destroyed. Tajik had gotten himself a black gun, but in Aziz's presence had twice been unable to summon the courage to use it.

Tajik had claimed to owe money to a half cousin who acted and dressed like a criminal. From now on, Aziz decided as he hurried back to the rendez- vous point, he would have to keep a close watch on Tajik. For his own good.

10

Dr. Hermann Ulm, armed with a rolled map, a sheaf of computer printout statistics and a fierce grin, confronted the Red Army major in charge of gunship operations in the Central Afghanistan theater.

"What I have here," the scientist said, approaching the officer's desk, "I know will please you."

Major Vlad Shirkov looked quite bored under his wild salt-and-pepper eyebrows. He sat behind a neat desk in an expansive office in Tajbeg Palace, which the Soviet military had converted into Command HQ Kabul. His broad hands, short fingers interlocked, rested on the desk blotter.

The old man put the printouts to one side, then unrolled the map across the blotter. "Thanks to Afghan Secret Police, we now have the location of the main mujahedeen stronghold pinpointed."

Major Shirkov pulled his hands out from under the map and laced his stumpy fingers behind his crew-cut head.

"It is there," Ulm continued, tapping the X drawn on the topographic map. "That is the entrance to the main complex of caves. My plan to destroy them and render them permanently unusable by the enemy is as follows. I need twenty MI-24 gunships. Five of these will carry rockets bearing Soman II gas warheads. Eight will carry one hundred of your best chemwar troopers in full protective gear. Seven will serve to provide covering and support fire against the fortified gun emplacements around and above the cave entrance. The gunships will launch their gas rockets into the mouth of the cave, then all helicopters will break off the attack and circle out of range of the position's guns. After a twenty-minute pause to give the nerve agent a chance to work its way deep into the cave system, the attack group will return and dispatch ground troops. These troops will enter the stronghold and verify that all the mujahedeen present are dead. If some small isolated pockets of resistance do still exist, the ground troops will eliminate them."

The major dismissed the proposal out of hand. "The risk is too great," he said.

Ulm could feel his blood pressure skyrocket. He was suddenly flush faced and in his ears there was a steady high ringing. "Risk? What risk?"

"We have already lost too many gunships in that sector," Shirkov said, jabbing at the X on the map.

"Even if your information on the precise location is accurate, the weather at that altitude can turn sour in minutes. We could face concentrated enemy antiaircraft fire without being able to launch."

Ulm smiled. He had the perfect answer. "There will be a radar homing beacon placed outside the entrance. If the weather closes in, the gunships can lock on the beacon."

"Are the final results in on Soman II?" the major said, quickly changing tack.

Dr. Ulm reached for the sheaf of printouts. "No," he said, "but these preliminary findings show—"

"Wait a minute," Shirkov said, putting up a hand. "You know what would happen to those one hundred troopers if they tried to enter the cave and the gas hadn't worked. They would be annihilated."

"The gas does work!" Ulm protested, waving the computer analysis in his face.

Shirkov again put his hands behind his head. "Until all the data from the village experiment is correlated, I cannot authorize the use of aircraft or troops under my command."

Ulm snatched back his printouts, rolled up his map.

"Sorry I can't assist you at the present time," the major said.

Ulm stormed out of the office. He knew damn well why the man wouldn't give the go-ahead for the attack. Shirkov was scared. Scared of making a decision, regardless of the facts that demanded it be made. He was scared not only of being wrong, but of being right, as well, of showing up the people above him in the chain of command. One did not get ahead in the military bureaucracy by being too bright or too successful. It was a familiar theme. It had been the same story in Ulm's Nazi Germany. Look what they'd done to Rommel.

The system's real crime, as Ulm saw it, was that the logic and power of pure scientific thought was inevitably chained to the petty maneuverings of uneducated, unsophisticated minds. If he had been allowed by the Nazi war planners to complete his work on ACHE inhibitors, there never would have been a Stalingrad, a disastrous retreat from the Russian winter. The soldiers of the Waffen SS would have marched unresisted all the way to China. But, no, they had to kill a few Jews—that was the priority.

This time Dr. Ulm was determined not to lose to a myopic establishment. He would persist doggedly until he was given the chance to show what his brainchild could accomplish.

11

Barrabas scanned the starry sky for a hint of dawn.

There was none.

His bones ached; his butt ached. The endless night ride out of Peshawar had been pure hell. For hours they had ridden straight into the teeth of a cold and wicked desert wind. Three times they had gotten wet to the hips while fording streams.

It was even colder now, in the last half hour before dawn. It was the time of day that made even a young man feel old.

Barrabas gritted his teeth as once again a calf muscle cramped tight. He shifted position on the worn saddle. It creaked under him as he leaned over to work out the cramp. The Afghan horse turned its head to the side and looked back at him with one eye. It was only faintly curious.

"It's okay, Old Floss," the white-haired man said softly, patting the animal on the neck. "Don't mind me. I'm just along for the ride."

The sturdy horse snorted and plodded steadily on without any urging from its rider. It had been to

Kabul and back many times before, carrying all types of baggage.

Ahead of Barrabas, Naazmomad rode point. Over one shoulder he had slung his .303 Enfield, over the other, in a leather pouch, his Koran. Behind Barrabas, the rest of the SOBs were strung out on similar mounts, with an occasional mule bearing gear tethered between.

The line of pack horses moved with a lethargy born of the knowledge that the sooner they got to their destination, the sooner they would have to make the trek back. They were surefooted, though. Even at night they were able to pick their way across boulder-strewn dry riverbeds, to edge along narrow cliff-side trails.

None of Barrabas's mercenaries had complained about being cold and wet. Or about the speed of the horses. The dangers of a night march through primitive terrain were all natural: a fatal fall, landslide, drowning. It seemed the "atheist invaders," as Naazmomad called them, had no stomach for night patrol in boondocks contested by the mujahedeen; they prized the current location of their balls too highly for that. After dark the brave Russians hid in their forts, manned their spotlights and heavy MGs and shot strings of tracers at anything that moved, in or out of range.

The dangers of the day along the rebel supply route were of an altogether different order. And the day was beginning to break, stars fading and purple light hitting the very tips of the snow-covered peaks above them.

His cramp massaged away, Barrabas straightened in the saddle. The Soviets worked at cutting the mujahedeen supply and reinforcement routes only from dawn to dusk and only with air power—MiG 21s and Hind gunships. Naazmomad had already given them the litany. Hear a MiG coming, get the horse in the shade of a tree or a rock. Hear a gunship coming, forget the horse, jump off and get under the damned rock. The jets moved too fast to pick out scattered, small, partially concealed targets; on the other hand, the armored attack helicopters, if given the opportunity, could climb right up your nose.

Ahead of Barrabas, their guide spurred on his horse. When it picked up speed, breaking into a brisk walk, the following horses automatically moved faster, as well. They were not in a good place to meet the dawn. For miles in all directions was a vast boulder field. There wasn't a tree in sight. And none of the rocks on the dusty ground was big enough to hide the horses behind; they were hardly big enough to hide a man. Naazmomad headed them for a line of hills in the distance.

The colonel turned on his saddle to look back at the SOBs. Lee was right behind him. She smiled with her eyes. The rest of her face was concealed under a native turban and muffler affair to keep out the wind. Behind her, the others were all wide awake and ready for anything.

When they were near enough to the hills to see their red color to recognize them as volcanic bedrock, stream and wind eroded into a maze of steepsided badlands, they heard a noise. Over the clump of their horseshoes came the sound of rotors beating, then the whap-whap-whap of cannon fire. It was heading toward them and fast.

Naazmomad signaled for the column to halt. They were still a quarter mile from cover, and that cover was in the direction the gunships were coming from. Before the guide could lower his hand, men came running out of a cut in the hills.

At least one hundred of them.

"Holy shit!" Nanos groaned.

Barrabas agreed with the Greek's assessment. The men were unarmed. Fresh recruits to the rebel cause, they had been heading south to Pakistan for training and to ferry back much-needed supplies. They now ran for their lives, spreading out across the deadly open ground. Over the top of the hills two Hinds appeared, in yellow and green camouflage warpaint, blood red Soviet stars on their tails. The muzzles of gunship cannons winked orange, and bursts of auto-fire rang across the broad wash. The running men were toppled and tossed by heavy caliber hits.

It was no contest.

Naazmomad shouted curt and frantic instructions at Barrabas and the others. In his excitement he shouted in a muddle of slang. Then he cried out to his God, and to the SOBs' utter shock, viciously spurred his horse, charging full gallop right at the oncoming helicopters.

"Yeeee-hah!" Billy Two whooped. "Would you look at that crazy little bastard go!"

"Dis-mount!" Barrabas yelled at them. There was no time to waste. "Get out your weapons and scatter!"

Gunship rotors beat the air; gunship cannons beat the earth. The Hind crews slaughtered the pedestrians methodically, hovering for a second or two, then shifting position to get the best angles of fire on the men trying to hide behind rocks the size of beach balls. The rebel recruits dissolved in a flurry of pulverized stone and exploding metal fragments.

Barrabas jumped from his horse, jerking his LAW 80 from its tie-down behind the saddle and across the horse's rump. He slapped the animal hard on the rear end and it bolted away. When he looked back to the massacre, it was already over. There had been nothing he or the SOBs could do to prevent it. They were too far away to provide effective cover to the runners. Only one person still moved on the plain in front of them.

Naazmomad rode back like a wild man over the broken ground, both Hinds in hot pursuit.

Barrabas discarded the LAW's protective end caps and extended the projectile tube, which unfolded the blast shield and shoulder rest as well as armed and cocked the weapon. He dropped to one knee just as a hail of cannon rounds sparked the stones all around him. Naazmomad was only thirty meters away and coming fast. The Hinds flew directly behind horse and rider, whipping up a maelstrom of white dust. Because the guide was riding straight for him, Barrabas couldn't shoot from a low angle. He cursed as he rose to his feet and shouldered the weapon. He ignored the aiming-shot capability of the LAW 80. There was no time for a goddamn aiming shot. The lead gunship was too close. When he looked through the optical sight he could see the pilot's face. He needed a shave. The colonel let the Afghan guide sweep past before he tightened down on the trigger.

As Naazmomad galloped madly by him, Barrabas swore he could hear the man laughing. Then the LAW shuddered and bucked on his shoulder. Ignition.

It was a point-blank shot.

The lead Hind took a 94 mm HEAT warhead through the windshield. The shaped charge detonated with a rocking explosion that blew out the entire cockpit. The dead gunship hurtled on over

Barrabas's head, carried by its own momentum, then nose-dived into the wash. Barrabas was slammed by the rush of dust as he turned to look behind him. In the middle of a swirling haze, the downed Hind's main rotors slashed at the earth, jerking the burning fuselage around behind it. Then the whole works exploded in a ball of flame.

Naazmomad grabbed his arm from behind and pulled him away as the remaining gunship made a strafing run on them. The two of them dived for the scant cover of the boulders.

"You turn! You turn!" Naazmomad yelled at him, unslinging both his rifle and his Koran.

"My turn? For what?"

Answering small-arms' fire from the rest of the SOBs whined overhead, clanging off the armored skin of the remaining MI-24. The Hind's pilot ignored it and them, banked sharply and began a second run on Barrabas and Naazmomad.

The guide's dark eyes danced in his hairy face. "I bring gunship for you kill. Now you bring gunship for me kill."

The image of the little Afghan riding hell-bent for leather in front of a pair of Soviet helicopters suddenly took on a new meaning. "I'll be god-damned!" Barrabas said, scrambling to his feet.

"That way! That way!" the guide told him, waving his arm to one side.

The colonel took off running just as the Hind swept down. He weaved and juked around the boulders, through the choking dust and clouds of black smoke from the fallen MI-24, drawing the attacking ship off the guide's position. Naazmomad wanted a broadside shot, Barrabas thought, skidding to a stop on a bed of loose stones, and he was damn well going to get one.

As the gunship overflew him, the white-haired man cut left and sprinted flat out, no evasive tactics. Above and behind him the Hind turned to pursue.

Barrabas could see Naazmomad in prone position, his SMLE shouldered. "Do it!" he shouted as the ground erupted in singing steel and hissing shards of rock.

The rifle barked once.

Then again and again, as the Afghan expertly worked the short throw bolt, dispensing a flow of one-and-a-half-second shots. The impact of the bullets did not make the clanging noise of a ricochet off armor but the solid thunk, thunk, thunk of penetration. Naazmomad was shooting for the big red star, which the Soviets had conveniently placed over the only unarmored part of the gunship, right over the turbine fuel pump.

The Hind's engine sputtered, gasped, died. Still firing, the ship suddenly veered away from its running human target, out of control as it lost power, as rotors slowed.

Naazmomad cheered, thrusting his vintage rifle up at the sky, even as the multimillion-dollar weapon of war plummeted.

The MI-24 landed flat on its belly, bounced twice, then lay still. The smell of spilled fuel hit Barrabas and Naazmomad at almost the same instant it all ignited. One of the crewmen must have already been at the door and had it open; the explosion blew the door and him out of the helicopter. His body flew twenty meters, then slammed headfirst into a rock.

As the SOBs rushed up, Naazmomad waved at them and proudly held up four fingers. For the four Hinds he had now brought down.

"I take it all back," Billy Two said, wringing the little man's callused hand. "You can shoot for my team any day."

"God is great," the guide said, grinning. Then he slipped around the huge Indian and moved off from the rest.

"Hey, where's he going?" Beck asked.

Naazmomad headed straight for the body of the gunship crewman. As he did so he drew out his knife.

"To collect two ears and a tail," Nanos said.

12

Gunther Dykstra sat in the shade of the dead scrub tree, watching the panorama of no-man's-land below the SOBs' temporary camp. Afghanistan was not a big country, but it was Big Country: like Arizona or New Mexico, it had spectacular if brutally rugged scenery. Gunther picked up his binoculars and glassed the face of a line of black cliffs ten kilometers away. With all the heat rising off the rocks, it was hard to be sure nothing man-sized was moving.

The smell of the cook fire behind him made the Dutchman grimace. His innards gurgled, rumbled and hissed with a grandeur that matched the view. Dr. Lee had given him some medicine for his intestinal problem. It had worked on the most unpleasant symptom of his malady, seizing his bowels up like concrete. But his belly still roiled.

At the thought of eating Naazmomad's chow, Gunther broke out in a cold sweat. He had seen the stringy chicken before it had gone into the pot. The guide had bought it from refugees traveling south.

A year of slow simmering would not tenderize that particular bird. Still, the guide's flavorless chicken and gritty rice were a vast improvement over his mutton stew. The sheep meat found therein wasn't just tough—it had a distinctive taste that was purely vile. But that wasn't the worst part. The worst part was the hard white mutton fat the dish contained. The congealed grease was so sticky and thick that it made the tongue cleave to the roof of the mouth. To free the tongue for its normal functions, one had to consume weak tea-flavored hot water drawn from some irrigation ditch. The hot water helped to melt the adhering fat. It also served to make one's guts home to assorted hostile flora and fauna.

Gunther scanned the bluff again. He had no one to blame but himself for the provisions. He could have arranged for TV dinners al fresco.

Something glinted low in the binoculars' field. He lowered them and swept the binoculars slowly back and forth. All he saw were rocks, rocks, rocks and the occasional dead tree.

The smells from behind were stronger. Soon he would have to face up to dinner. It was a trick of the mind, of course, but it felt like his belly was already getting more distended. He lowered the glasses, undid the top button of his trousers and got immediate relief.

With his naked eye he saw the flash this time. Stomach troubles forgotten, he peered through the binoculars. A gunsight dropped behind a rock. It reappeared on the other side. And continued on. It was a Kalashnikov sight.

Gunther swept ahead of the moving gun, up a gulley he could now make out, because now he knew it had to be there. The gulley led right up to the camp.

He put down the glasses and took hold of the eighty-meter length of fine-gauge wire between himself and the other SOB. He gave the wire two hard pulls and felt it come up tight each time. It was the signal that they had company.

Gunther was confident that the alarm signal would not go unnoticed. The other end of the wire was tied to Liam O'Toole's thumb.

DR. LEONA HATTON HAD DECIDED that after three and a half days on the trail, she needed a bath more urgently than she needed food. Especially Naazmomad's food. She left the other SOBs sitting around the cook fire and followed upstream the little river they were camped beside. The river was impossible to miss; it was outlined by the only green in the landscape. It meandered through a layer of bedrock, gouging potholes in the softer spots. She walked until she discovered a small pool about the size of a bathtub.

Lee looked around. She was well out of sight of the other mercenaries. When she stuck a hand in the water, she jerked it quickly back. "Oh, my God!" she gasped. The stream was from a mountain spring and ice cold.

Still, it was the only bath in town.

Lee set her soap down on a rock and took off her boots, then unwound the turban from her short black hair. The ethnic headgear served as a protective disguise for her. Women in the outback were not supposed to wear pants, and she was damned if she'd go to war in a *chadri*, so she had done her best to avoid looking like a woman.

The lady doctor took off her shoulder holster and the Smith hogleg it held. After unfastening the holster's hammer strap, she carefully laid gun and holster in the shade of a bush. The rest of her clothes went into a neat pile on a boulder at the water's edge.

"Ohhhhhhh," she groaned as she put a bare foot in the pool. The ache was instant and went clear to the bone. She drew her foot back, muttering under her breath. She was determined to have a bath, no matter how much pain and suffering it caused her or how short it was in duration. Gritting her teeth, Lee strode quickly into the center of the clear, sandy-bottomed pool and sat in the shallow water.

For a second.

It was so cold that it took her breath away.

She jumped straight up, clutching herself, then hopped about, almost losing her balance.

"At least you're wet," she said through chattering teeth. Now the bone ache was all the way to her knees; that was the height of the water. She rubbed the bar of soap briskly against her skin, trying to work up a lather. The water was so hard it barely yielded any suds.

"To hell with it," she said, throwing the bar of soap up on the bank after a couple of minutes. Having done the best she could under the circumstances, again she sat. This time she bent at the waist and put her face under, as well.

She lasted another second or so before the temperature drove her abruptly to her feet. She shuddered and blinked water out of her eyes.

Three strange men in native costume stood not fifteen meters from her, on the side of the river where her clothes were stacked. They all had full, greasy beards, grimy fezs and grins from ear to ear.

"Oh, shit," Lee groaned, trying in vain to cover her nudity with her hands. Only one of the men was armed with a gun, a battered folding-stock AK, the other two had knives with fancy scabbards and handles hanging from their belts. "Why don't you be nice boys and hand me my clothes?" she asked in English.

One of the tribesmen, a narrow-shouldered fellow with small, close-set eyes, picked up her man's trousers, sniffed at them, then tossed them to his buddies. He picked up her panties and held them in front of himself, as if testing them for size.

"Come on, don't fool around, okay?" Lee said.

The tribesman with the AK picked up her bra with the front sight and waved it back and forth like a flag. As he did this he looked her body over and made kissing sounds with his mouth.

"You've got to be kidding," Lee told him.

He wasn't. He said something to the other two and while he took a front row seat on a rock, they came after her, jumping right into the water.

Before they could grab her, Lee ran the other way, scrambling out of the pool, looking around frantically for some kind of weapon. She found one. She snatched up a dead tree branch about a meter long and whirled to face her pursuers.

"Does it still look good to you?" she asked, wielding the thick, crooked club over her shoulder like a baseball bat.

The tribesmen laughed at her, made more kissing sounds and put out their hands as if to pinch and tweak. They were having the time of their lives. The guy on the rock said something to them. Evidently he was the tactical expert. The two tribesmen moved away from each other, spreading out so they could come at her from both sides at once.

Lee made sure she had solid footing under her. It was the key to a home-run ball. When the two of them charged, they did so with their arms outstretched. She didn't know how many defenseless women these guys had attacked, but one thing was sure: they had never run into one like her before.

She pivoted and swung at the man on her right. Not high at his head or neck, but low, at the knee. She swung so hard that the club hissed as it arched through the air. She caught the tribesman on the outer edge of the left kneecap and felt the jolting impact all the way to her shoulder. Something crunched. Her expertise in Escrima, Filipino stick fighting, and in human physiology told her the kneecap was not merely cracked, but shattered like a china saucer. The tribesman let out a shrill shriek and went down howling, clutching his leg.

The man with the beady eyes took the opportunity to grab her firmly by the shoulders. Lee rammed the butt of the club back and up into his groin. He made a strangled sound and let go at once. When she turned, his knees were already giving way and his face was a curious shade of purple. She gave him one more for good measure, winding up and bashing him across the side of the head, putting him down on his face in the dirt.

The man sitting on the rock pointed his AK at her belly and snarled something unintelligible at her. It was clear he wasn't pleased by the terrible accidents that had befallen his pals. But his concern for their well-being was tempered by the needs of libido. He gestured sharply at the ground at his feet, made an unmistakable "spread 'em" gesture and meaningfully untied the woven sash of his trousers.

Lee walked slowly through the frigid pool, her hands at her sides. The game was over. In hand to hand, or stick to hand, the object was to incapacitate the enemy, to do so with exactly the right amount of force so as to inflict only the damage required. Firearms were not such precision tools. To play with them was to play for keeps. She didn't look once at the Smith in the bush. She knew right where it was, though. And she knew the ivory grip was facing her.

When the tribesman stood up, she dived for the hidden pistol. As she landed on her bare belly, her right hand closed on the big Smith's butt. The man above swung his assault rifle down on her. There was no time to free the gun from its sheath. She raised both gun and holster and from a prone position fired twice, double action, right through the leather.

The first bullet was a bit low, striking the man in the abdomen. He never felt the second; it hit him above the bridge of the nose. His head snapped back from the impact and a slurry of brains and blood splashed over the dusty stones. He collapsed onto his back, toppling over the stone that had been his seat. Only his booted feet were visible. They stuck up in the air. They did the dance.

Lee jerked the Smith out of the flaming holster and dunked the holster in the pool.

From behind her came running feet. She turned and assumed the Weaver stance.

"Holy shit, Doc!" Nanos said, looking at the muzzle of the chromed .44 Magnum she was pointing at him, at her nakedness, then at the various sprawled men.

Lee lowered the weapon.

"Why doesn't this ever happen to you, Alex?" she said, stepping out of the pool and reaching for her clothes.

"It does," he assured her, moving over to examine the unconscious tribesman with the muzzle of his AK. "Hey, I swear I can't go into a Third World restaurant anymore without getting jumped by half the waiters and all the busboys."

The Greek straightened up. "This guy's gonna sleep for a week. The one over there, he's going sleep until Joshua blows his horn."

"Who are they?" Beck said, approaching the writhing member of the trio.

"Soldiers of Allah," said a gruff male voice.

The announcement was accompanied by a rustle in the bushes along the river and a clattering sound, like thirty or so metal crickets clicking.

Kalashnikov crickets.

Beck, Nanos and Hatton got their guns up.

Not that it was much comfort.

They were outnumbered ten to one.

Then Barrabas and the rest of the SOBs showed up. It was a face-off between the two armed groups.

Naazmomad stepped to the front and spoke to the leader of the tribesmen. He kept his rifle belt-high, aimed, and his finger on the trigger.

"I am Ahmad Yar," the gray-bearded headman said. "I speak English. You speak English."

Barrabas put a hand on the guide's shoulder. "What seems to be your problem, Ahmad Yar?" he asked, though he already knew the answer. The Afghan rebel movement was fraught with feuding factions. *Badal*, or blood for blood, did not only apply to the atheist invaders.

"You cross the territory of the Jamiat-I-Islamis, therefore you must pay a toll."

Liam O'Toole glanced at the bodies around the pool. He grinned at Yar over the sights of his AK. "Looks like you're the ones who paid the toll, Buckwheat."

"I will take your black guns," Ahmad Yar said. "I will take your ammunition. And I will take the woman."

"You will take shit," Lee said, thumbing back the hammer on the Smith. It made a hard click. She drew a bead on the headman's chin.

Weapons on both sides of the little river were quickly shouldered. The tension jumped up a couple of notches.

"Do you think a few guns are worth it?" Barrabas asked the leader of the Jamiat-I-Islamis.

"Worth what?"

"You're going to lose more than half your men," the colonel told him. "That's a guarantee."

The Afghan's eyes narrowed as he surveyed the line of men opposing him. They were not soft, weak like the Russian donkeys; they were trained warriors, prepared to kill or be killed at a word, at a single false move.

"Of those men," the white-haired man went on, "one is going to be you. Also guaranteed."

"There is glory in dying for Allah," Ahmad Yar said.

"What about dying for nothing?" Barrabas said.

Claude Hayes broke in. "It will be for worse than nothing. We are all fighting for the same cause."

"So you come to kill Russians?" the headman asked the black soldier of fortune. "Who do you try to fool? There are no Westerners helping us fight for our freedom. No foreign mercenaries. The free governments of the world supply us with guns, but they let us do our own dying."

"We are here," Liam said. "And if you don't think we're ready to die, just try us."

"I think the best thing for both of us to do under the circumstances is to back up," Barrabas said. "And keep backing up until we're out of each other's range."

Ahmad Yar considered the proposal, then nodded agreement. The tribesmen picked up their wounded.

"Everybody, take one step back," the colonel said.

When the two groups were a hundred meters apart, the step-for-step thing disintegrated. The Jamiat-I-Islamis turned their backs on the SOBs and sauntered off across the plain.

"Man, I'm glad that's over," Lee said, rubbing the knots out of her forearms. The Smith was heavy.

"It not over," Naazmomad said.

"What do you mean?" Beck asked.

"We come back this way."

13

It took the nine-person column of mercenaries on horseback almost an hour to traverse the series of ascending switchbacks. When they reached a saddle between a pair of low, craggy peaks, Naazmomad reined up his mount and signaled for a stop. As he jumped down from his horse he waved for Barrabas and Liam to follow him to the edge of the rocky ridge.

It was the evening of the fourth day of the trek. It had taken longer than anticipated because they had made a wider swing around Kabul than planned, to avoid Afghan army patrols. If they maintained their current course and rate of progress, the target was still one full day away.

The colonel and O'Toole joined the guide, dropping to their bellies beside him, peering over the ridge top. Some five hundred meters below, they saw a small barren valley backed by steep-sided mountains. In the fading purple light, the peaks cast long shadows across the plain of stones.

"You see there?" Naazmomad said, pointing at the north end of the valley. He indicated a pass between the sheer mountain walls.

A pass guarded by a pair of Soviet main battle tanks.

"T-72s," Liam said, lowering his binoculars.

"We go that way," Naazmomad said, pointing again at the tanks.

"Can't we go around them?" Barrabas asked, making a sweeping gesture with his arm.

Naazmomad shook his head. "Go around take six, maybe seven more days. Go that way."

"That means killing the tanks," Barrabas said.

The guide grinned, shouldered an imaginary LAW and nodded eagerly.

"What do you think, Liam?"

The Irish-American scanned the intervening terrain, then the tanks. "I think he's right, we got no choice. Here, you have a look." He handed the field glasses to Barrabas. "The way they've got themselves backed into the pass," he continued, "they're set to cover the whole valley floor with their main armament, those 125 mm smooth-bore cannons."

"I see that."

"That's not the worst part of it, either. Both tanks are equipped with nightsights. You can see the infrared searchlight on the right side of the main gun. To the left of the gunner's hatch is a panoramic day-nightsight. They are going to be impossible to sneak past."

"They are also facing us," Barrabas said. "If we have to take them head-on like that, the LAW HEAT warheads won't be able to penetrate the glacis, the sloped, armored front of the tank. That incline on the nose gives eighty-millimeter-thick armor the protective capability of five or six hundred millimeters."

Naazmomad pulled Barrabas's arm and indicated a narrow shadow running the length of the valley. It was a shallow gulley, almost invisible in any other light. "After dark we go there. Go slow. Get close." He smacked his fist into his open palm. "Pow!"

"Dirty job for four or five guys," Liam said.

"I know just the four," Barrabas told him.

They withdrew from the edge of the ridge and rejoined the others.

"In about an hour we're going to start down the hill," Barrabas announced. "Four of us are going to cross the plain down there and destroy the two tanks guarding the pass entrance. The rest of you will wait with the horses and gear until you hear the 'go' signal—three spaced shots, followed by three more. When you get the signal, hightail it to the pass. If you don't hear it, the tanks are still there and the four won't be coming back. The order, then, is to go around. To fulfill the mission accordingly to plan, if possible.''

"Who's going to get to go on this little tank hunt?" Billy Two said.

"Myself, Beck, Hayes and you."

"But, Colonel—" Liam protested.

"No arguments."

O'Toole shut up. He had been fighting alongside the white-haired man on and off for almost ten years. Ten years of undeclared wars, ''unstable'' areas, wildass free-fire zones where friends and enemies swapped allegiances between magazine changes. From the start of their business relationship, from day one, Nile Barrabas had been the boss. He knew how to get things done that nobody else would even tackle. He didn't put a higher value on his own life than on the lives of the men under him. It was one of the reasons he could get hardbitten soldiers of fortune to follow him into battle. The main reason, however, was that he didn't make mistakes in judgment—even in, especially in, the heat of battle. It was a knack, a gift that O'Toole envied and respected.

Three hours later the SOBs were gathered at the foot of the mountain they had descended.

"Night's too damn clear," Liam grumbled.

Overhead the stars were out in profusion, and a quarter moon spread a ghastly pale light over the stony plain.

"They'll be able to see you guys without infrared," O'Toole went on.

"Not if we keep our butts down," Beck replied. "And I, for one, intend to do just that."

"Let's move out," the colonel said. With that he took point, crossing a short stretch of open ground in a running crouch, his LAW 80 strapped to his back, his AK in his hands. He jumped into the gulley and waited for the others to catch up.

When Hayes, Beck and Billy Two were beside him, he started moving north along the gulley.

It was rough going. The ditch was only four feet deep and keeping one's butt and head down meant hopping boulders and deadfalls hunched over. The quartet moved silently, except for the soft, rasping sound of their breathing. All their gear was battened down, rattle and rustle proof.

They made a stop halfway along.

Barrabas spoke in a whisper. "Use your spotting rifles first, no matter how close you are," he reminded them. He had no qualms about making doubly sure they had the routine straight. He knew from hard experience that even seasoned professionals could get buck fever when facing down fifty-plus tons of enemy tank. "Don't take a head-on shot, no matter what. It will just be a wasted round. The armor's too thick. Get a side shot and the right side if you can manage it. The main fuel cells are along the hull on that side. Or hit the gun turret. It's conventional cast armor. A HEAT warhead should make a nice, neat hole in it. When we get to the end of the line, we split up. Beck and me will take the T-72 on the left. You two take the one on the right. Give us the first shot because it'll take us a little longer to get into position. You guys have the green light as soon as we cut loose. Understood?''

Heads nodded.

The four men resumed their crab-walk until they reached the point where the gulley turned into a broad cleft in the mountainside. Barrabas peeked over the gulley rim. They were sixty meters from the right-hand tank, one hundred meters from the one on the left. Plenty close enough in either case to take a killing shot, if the angle of attack were not so bad. He sat back down, checked his watch's luminous dial, then raised three fingers to the others. They would rest for a few minutes, stretch their legs and prepare to make the final assault.

Beck took a quick look, too. He could see the T-72s lying in wait in the dark: squat, huge, silent. The moonlight glinted off their flat camo paint job. Each had a 125 mm gun turned to face front and, mounted on the commander's cupola, facing to the rear, a 12.7 mm antiaircraft machine. All the hatches were shut tight.

Like sleeping monsters, Beck thought, drawing back to the suddenly insignificant, even ridiculous, cover of the ditch. The tanks made his skin crawl. He was scared spitless, but refused to surrender to his fear.

When Barrabas gave the signal to leave the gulley, Beck's legs were all squishy in the knees. They moved at his command, but sluggishly as if half-asleep. Heart pounding, he followed the colonel up onto the plain. They had to cross directly in front of both tanks to get into position for taking a straight perpendicular shot at their target.

They had gone roughly half the necessary distance when the night's silence was broken by the sound of an electric motor, a high-pitched whirring. Beck glanced over his shoulder and saw the left-hand tank turret rotating slowly in their direction. It was scanning the plain.

Barrabas saw it, too. Both mercenaries had the same realization in the same instant: they weren't going to make it to the other side. The white-haired man dropped to his belly. So did Nate Beck.

Though Beck couldn't see it, he knew the infrared searchlight was on. When the turret motor suddenly shut down, he held his breath. He felt like a bug on a pin. Was the tank crew looking at him through their panoramic sight and laughing? Were they drawing lots to see who got to cut the intruders to ribbons? Then the motor started up again. Beck looked back and saw the turret moving back to its original position.

In front of him, Barrabas was already on his feet and moving. Beck hurried to catch up.

If he hadn't been in such a hurry, he would have seen the pothole. If he had seen the pothole, he wouldn't have fallen flat on his face directly in front of the right-hand tank. A large, pointed rock jabbed up into his stomach as he landed and his own weight drove the air from his lungs; it forced a loud and unfortunate "Ooooof!" from his throat.

To his right, both turrets whirred.

He rolled onto his back, gasping.

The monsters had awakened.

The 780-horsepower diesels roared and the tank closest to Beck lurched forward on its twelve wheels and double tracks, lumbering right at him. It was a nightmare come to life. Nate didn't even have time to turn onto his stomach. The nose of the tank loomed over him, shutting off the light of the stars. The earth shook beneath him as metal treads supporting fifty thousand tons of metal rolled onward. The underside of the tank's hull covered him. Smothered him. He just might have screamed at that point. If he had, he couldn't even hear it himself over the bellow of the huge engine. He was sure he was about to be crushed, mangled to death by the tracks, sucked up into the grinding drive wheels. Or if Barrabas shot a rocket with him trapped under the tank, he'd burn alive with the tank crew.

Barrabas did not fire. He had seen the skinny little man disappear under the belly of the T-72.

Like a wave of clanking madness, the armored vehicle passed over Nate Beck, its underhull grazing his chest. It left him blinking once more up at the heavens.

He could hear the turret motor's whine. It was turning, following the direction the colonel had gone. Beck rolled to his feet. He needed more distance between himself and his target. He needed it quick. Beck left his AK in the dirt and ran another ten meters before kneeling and shouldering the LAW 80.

As he did so, machine gunfire erupted from the front of the tank. Cordite flicker-flash strobed the near mountainside. They had Barrabas pinned behind a rock pile.

But not for long.

The tall, white-haired man darted out from the stone shield, LAW on his shoulder.

Pow-ping! Pow-ping! Nine-millimeter spotting rounds clanged off the tank's armored hull. Then hard yellow-white light flared out of the darkness and the tank rocked as it took a HEAT warhead amidships. Beck was momentarily blinded by the flash, stunned by the shock blast. In afterimage he could see a kneeling man between two blazing ends of LAW tube at the moment of launch. He rubbed his eyes to clear them.

The wounded tank's engine howled as it tried to maneuver. Its treads made a horrible screeching sound, mangled road wheels unable to advance it. The tank to Beck's right, seeing that its partner was in desperate trouble, began to advance, MG firing as it did so.

If the crippled monster could not move forward, it could still rotate its turret. And it could still shoot. Its PKT machine gun spat 7.62 x 39 mm rounds at Barrabas, who dived back to the cover of the heap of rock.

Beck fired a spotting round, plinking it off the side of the turret. Then he unleashed his rocket. The rearward blast of ignition-and-burn gusted the rocks twenty meters behind him for an instant, then the 94 mm projectile was long gone. The shaped-charge warhead slammed the turret, punching a hole through it just below the bulge of the commander's cupola. It stopped rotating at once.

Behind Beck two more LAW rockets exploded and the other tank burst into flames. Hayes and Starfoot had done their job.

It was no longer dark in the little valley. A bonfire fueled by one thousand gallons of diesel leaped toward the stars; a pall of foul black smoke shifted, drifted across the moonscape plain.

To Beck's astonishment the commander's hatch of the other tank suddenly flipped back open and a man in a flame-retardant jump suit and head gear popped out. He grabbed the operating handle of the 12.7 mm antiaircraft machine gun, swung it around and opened fire on Barrabas. The heavier slugs chewed the covering of rocks to powder.

Beck knew that unless he did something, and quickly, the colonel was going to be dog meat. He knelt only twenty meters from the surviving tank, close enough to hit the commander with a stone. Beck's AK lay half that distance from him, in the dirt where he had left it. He could never get to it in time.

He did not have to stop to throwing rocks, though.

He still had a weapon in his hands, albeit seriously reduced in caliber.

The spotting rifle.

He sighted on the tank commander and squeezed the trigger until the gun clicked on an empty chamber. He hit the man four times. Four 9 mm head shots.

The commander slumped over the gun, then the spilled fuel caught with a savage explosion. Beck was knocked flat on his butt by the roaring fireball. It was so close that it singed off his eyebrows.

Barrabas helped him to his feet as Hayes and Billy Two rushed over.

"I thought we were going to have to scrape you up with a spatula and take you home between a couple of sheets of waxed paper," Billy Two said.

"Yeah, you and me both," Beck said weakly. "That was some experience."

"You did a good job, Nate," Claude added, slapping him on the back. "You hung tough."

"Saved my bacon," the colonel said. "I owe you one, Mr. Beck."

"Who's ging to give the all-clear signal to the others?" Billy Two asked.

Barrabas turned to the smallest SOB and handed him an AK. "You do the honors, Nate."

Beck smiled broadly. He raised the assault rifle overhead and fired three spaced shots, followed by three more, and a war whoop.

14

It was not until late in the afternoon of the following day that the SOBs took position on a hilltop opposite and below their target. The old Mogul fort sat on the side of a gently sloping mountain, about 150 meters from the summit. The summit consisted of a jumble of jagged spires the fort's builders considered too narrow, too dangerous to support a serious threat to the security of the site.

The SOBs were separated from the mountain fortress by a valley gouged out aeons before by a retreating glacier. The depression between the two summits was broad, dish-shaped and canted at an angle that favored the fort. The distance involved was close to fifteen kilometers.

"The bastard who designed that dump wasn't dumb," O'Toole said. "Look at the distance from the valley floor to the perimeter walls. Must be five or six kilometers. A long way to charge uphill under fire without cover."

Barrabas agreed. The last part was the killer. No cover. The slope was bare rock, polished slick as glass by the tremendous pressure of the advancing and retreating ice. The only places it wasn't smooth were the scattered fans of loose rubble, glacial debris. A difficult path, any way you looked at it. To have moved men and equipment up it would have been almost impossible without winches and pulleys. And unlimited time.

The Soviets had used dynamite and bulldozers to scratch a road from the bedrock for their armored personnel carriers. It would back-and-forth a half dozen times below the huge main gates, then shot straight down the valley. With all the firepower they had assembled along the walls of the fort, the Soviets figured to control any frontal assault the ragamuffin mujahedeen could muster. Heavy Kalashnikov machine guns looked down from the fort's three towers, able to apply a beaten zone of 12.7 mm slugs any place on the slope. Barrabas could see the sight markers set at even intervals on the mountainside. They had the ranges already computed.

The idea of hijacking a BTR-60 and driving it into the fort was not as harebrained as it seemed. Short of parachuting into the central courtyard, it was the only way the SOBs were going to get in.

"Look, a patrol's coming out now," Claude said.

Three little vehicles exited the fort's main gate and began to creep down the mountain.

"Where will they go, Naazmomad?" Barrabas asked.

The guide pointed down to the valley floor, where a crude road wound around and between the boulder outcroppings, then south. "Patrol go that way, look for signs of mujahedeen. If find mujahedeen, call in gunships or MiG strike from Kabul before it get dark."

Barrabas watched the eight-wheeled, square-nosed personnel carriers through binoculars. They sported broad rear-entry gates. They were armed with one heavy and two light machine guns. The former was mounted in the middle of the vehicle's roof, above the driver's compartment; the latter were on the right and left side of the roof above the second set of wheels. A long whip antenna jutted up from the roofline to the left of the driver's compartment.

"We're going to have trouble with those three radios," Barrabas said.

"We don't want them to call in an air strike against us on the way up the hill," Liam said.

"But we do need an intact radio or we're never going to be able to get into the fort," Barrabas said. "It's going to be a touchy job, any way you cut it." He lowered the field glasses and turned to their guide. "Do you have a place in mind for the ambush?" he asked.

Naazmomad nodded. "Pair-fect," he said. "We be there ten minutes before the BTRs get there— plenty of time to get all ready."

"Okay," Barrabas said to the others, "let's get this circus on the road."

The mercenaries mounted their horses and followed Naazmomad's lead. He took them down the back side of the hill, then along a winding dry riverbed. Daylight was already beginning to fade and in the lengthening shadows of the canyon, the temperature had started to plummet.

The guide stopped at the point where the wash crossed the crude road.

Barrabas surveyed the terrain. There were three huge boulder outcrops that the road snaked around. Each was the size of a small house. The largest of the outcrops was in the middle of the kill zone. "You picked a good spot," he told Naazmomad. "I like the way the road cuts that deep channel through the bedrock. No way is one of those BTRs going to be able to turn out of the track, get up onto the slope and escape."

"What's the plan, Colonel?" Liam asked.

"You, Gunther and Nanos will take a position behind the middle, biggest rock," Barrabas said. "When the first BTR comes into view, stop it cold with a LAW rocket and take out any survivors."

"Gotcha," O'Toole said.

"Naazmomad, Hayes and Hatton will wait behind the first rock and hit the last BTR in line."

"What about the rest of us?" Billy Two said.

"Billy, you and me and Beck will take the middle BTR. That's the one we need intact. We also need all radio transmissions from it temporarily shut off."

"No sweat, Colonel," Beck said. "I can disconnect the antenna from the outside and reconnect it any time, any way you want."

"What if the guys in the middle tin can don't want to come out?" Nanos said. "I mean they could just sit in there and wait us out. Once morning comes they'll get all the air support they need."

"If they don't want to come out," Liam said, "we convince 'em it's in their best interest."

"Any more questions?" Barrabas asked.

There were none.

"Get in position."

"IF YOU WANT TO SHOOT IT, SHOOT IT," O'Toole said to Nanos as they crouched behind a cluster of car-sized smaller rocks. "I'm not going to sit here and argue with you about it."

"Hey, I don't care one way or the other," Gunther said.

"Well, if you guys insist," the Greek said through a mile-wide grin, picking up the antitank weapon. He opened the LAW's blast shield and shouldered the weapon, shifting position of his elbows on the rocks to get comfortable. "Don't stand behind me," he told the others, "unless you are seriously into third-degree burns."

"We know, we know," Gunther said.

"Just hit the target," Liam said.

He and Gunther got their extra AK mags all set out, made sure their cover behind the boulders was secure, that no ricochets could be skipped into them along flat planes of rock in front or to the side.

Behind the LAW, Nanos began to hum, annoyingly without tune. He stopped humming when they heard the sound of engines coming their way. He had already mentally rehearsed the sequence of his shots. The first would be a spotting round, set up to lead the BTR creeping around a tight burn. The second shot would be the real thing, go for broke, with altered lead, if the spotting round didn't strike where he wanted.

The BTR in question rounded the hairpin turn even slower than the Greek had anticipated.

"Hello, there," he said as he squeezed off the spotting round, his right eye pressed to the optical sight. The LAW 80's rifle barked and the bullet rang off the nose of the vehicle. Nanos cut down the speed of his swing.

The LAW rocket squealed and leaped from its tube.

From the point of view of Gunther, Liam and Nanos, it looked like the whole front left side of the BTR exploded. The concussion shook down a slide of loose rock from the slope above. The personnel carrier didn't stop. It rolled past the cloud of cordite smoke and the SOBs could see a hole punched through the driver's compartment. A HEAT warhead did nasty things to armor plate. Its shaped charge drove a concentrated wedge of force through the metal, blasting free bits of steel on the armor's inner surface, sending those bits jetting through anything and anyone inside the hull.

"Hey, who's in charge?" Nanos exclaimed as the BTR veered off the track.

As it rammed into the side of a large boulder, another rocket exploded, this one at the other end of the kill zone. The Greek's wounded BTR tried to climb the bungalow-size boulder. It got up to about a seventy-five-degree angle before it toppled and crashed onto its side, blocking the road from shoulder to shoulder, all eight wheels spinning.

"Neat, huh?" Nanos said, putting down the LAW and picking up his AK.

As he spoke, the rear gate of the overturned BTR powered open and a quintet of very angry Com-Bloc troopers rushed out, shooting from the hip. Steel-cored slugs whined off the rocks all around the SOBs' position. While Liam, Gunther and Nanos ducked for cover, the Soviets made it easily to the protection of the huge boulder.

"No, Nanos," O'Toole growled out of the side of his mouth as more steel cores kept them pinned noses to the dirt, "not neat at all."

HAYES HELD HIS BREATH, measuring the seconds between the rocket explosion at the other end of the trap and the appearance around the bend of the last BTR in lifetimes. If the third personnel carrier backed up, somehow got turned around, they were going to have hell to pay.

Then it was there, right in front of him, and he popped off a quick pair of spotting rounds, watching the dust and paint fly at the points of impact. He fired his LAW.

The rocket struck right over the two bright marks on the hull. Just below the splash guard, between the rear two sets of wheels.

Claude had hit the jackpot. The fuel cell.

The BTR boomed and belched fire from its rear end, still rolling under power.

The back gate began to lower, flames and smoke pouring out of the main compartment.

The vehicle crashed head-on into the largest boulder, fire shooting up from its view ports in three-meter plumes. The soldiers trapped inside tried to get out. Only two made it. The two closest to the rear gate. Human torches tumbled from the rear hatch of the BTR, then ran screaming down the crude road, flapping their arms.

"Mine," the Afghan guide said, tightening down on his Enfield's trigger. His rifle cracked sharply, and one of the burning troopers dropped as if all his strings had been cut. Naazmomad worked the bolt with precision, aimed and fired again. The second man crumpled onto his face before he reached the bend of the road, black smoke curling from his back.

The guide ejected the cartridge case, then picked it and the other brass up, showing them to Hayes and Hatton. "Two dollars United States," he said proudly, "two dead invaders." He clenched the cases in his brown fist.

"Definitely cost effective," Hayes said.

THE MIDDLE BTR SKIDDED to a stop an instant after the lead vehicle was hit. It stopped beside the biggest rock, whose smooth gray dome loomed over it.

According to plan, Nate Beck had meanwhile climbed atop the massive boulder. He looked straight down on the roof of the enemy personnel carrier. Gritting his teeth, linesman's cutting dikes in hand, AK strapped to his back, Beck let himself start to slide down the slick, curved face. After three meters he was in free fall.

He aimed for the middle of the BTR's roof, circling his arms to correct his downward flight. The roof came up fast and hard. He landed on his feet first, then rolled onto his side, dissipating the force of impact.

"Oh, Mama!" he moaned as the personnel carrier's heavy machine gun and the light MG on the left side pivoted toward the SOBs' position and clattered auto-fire simultaneously. All the BTR's armament could be operated remotely, from controls inside the vehicle.

He stepped toward the cab, behind the raging main MG, then onto the nose of the BTR. Through the small rectangular double front windows he could see the driver and the driver could see him. The Russian had on a fur-lined hat with ear flaps up and looked Mongolian. As Beck watched, the driver turned back to the passenger compartment and yelled something.

The light MG on the right, next to the boulder, couldn't turn far enough to the left to bring fire to bear on its enemies, but it could pivot enough to give Beck a hard time. As he knelt on the BTR's nose and reached out to clip the antenna lead, the 7.62 mm machine gun cut loose. Stuttering auto-fire slashed the air less than a foot over his head; the blazing muzzle was right in line with his face.

Close, but no cigar.

Knowing he couldn't be hit, seeing the furious faces inside the armored car made Nate feel downright cocky. He gave the Mongolian driver a one-finger salute. Then he moved farther to the right, beyond the arc of the light MG's fire path and behind the main gun, which was keeping Barrabas and Billy Two pinned down some twenty meters away.

He grabbed the stuttering 12.7 mm Kalashnikov by the receiver and tried to shift the point of aim with brute force. Maybe the Greek could have done it, but weighing 160 pounds wet, Beck found it impossible. The controls were hydraulic; he couldn't cut the tubing with his dikes because it was inside a mount made of three-inch pipe. There was only one thing he could do. The Soviets had designed the fire controls of the BTR well, but the top-mounted MGs were loaded by cannister from the outside. From the outside they could be likewise unloaded.

Beck unfastened the magazine and cut the plastic feed belts.

After a second or two the firing stopped.

Barrabas and Billy Two advanced at once, running toward the BTR low and fast. They were halfway there when the firing ports on the left side, behind front and back wheels, flipped up and a cluster of AKM muzzles poked out. The mercenaries hit the dirt as once again they were under fire. If there hadn't been so many ComBloc troopers trying to get a shot at them, and in the process knocking off each other's aim, they would have been killed in the first salvo.

Gun smoke poured from the open firing ports as Beck jumped to the edge of the roof. He quickly flipped the metal port doors back down and sat in front of one so it couldn't reopen. He could hear the occupants of the BTR hacking and coughing inside. There was a good reason why the designers of the armored vehicle had put its MGs on the outside. Ventilation. The inside of the BTR was now a miniature gas chamber, filled with toxic gunshot fumes.

Billy Two jumped up on the splash guard and sat on the BTR roof, pinning the other vent-firing port on the left side shut with his legs. He, too, could hear the coughing and moans from the trapped troopers.

"Now what?" the Indian asked the man with the white hair.

"WE GOT PLACES TO GO, things to do," Liam said as more ComBloc slugs chipped away at their position. "We can't be hanging around here all night."

"What do you suggest?" Nanos said.

"I'll hit 'em from the front and you two go around and flank 'em."

"Deal," Gunther said.

"On three..."

The Irish-American dashed from cover, across open ground, bullets clipping the rocks at his heels. He zigzagged his way to the side of the overturned BTR, then attempted to return aimed fire. The moment he stuck his AK muzzle around the end of the vehicle, a wall of steel cores slammed into it, forcing him to duck back. "Okay, screw you, too," he said, holding the assault rifle one-handed, thrusting it around the personnel carrier's bumper, shooting unaimed at his enemy.

Gunther and Nanos ran behind the boulder and stopped. The firing was almost all one way.

The wrong way.

"O'Toole was supposed to give us some covering fire." Nanos said.

Bullets whined off stone to the left.

"There he is," Gunther said. "Let's do it."

They charged the enemy hard position, firing short auto-bursts from the hip.

The hail of lead made the troopers duck, which gave O'Toole time to get set. He stepped out from behind the bulk of the vehicle and braced himself against the bumper. When the Russians popped up again, Liam popped off aimed fire. He killed two with clean single head shots.

Gunther and Nanos overran the other three. Triggers pinned, clattering breeches spewing arcs of brass, they chopped the invaders down. One of them was trying to reload at the crucial instant. He looked up helplessly from his empty AK as the Greek vaulted a big rock in front of him. A line of sudden death stitched across his chest and he slumped beside his thrashing fellows.

Gunther ejected an empty mag and cracked in a fresh one. Nanos did the same as O'Toole ran up.

"Nice work," he said, surveying the carnage. "Let's go check out how the others did."

"TELL 'EM TO THROW all their weapons out the rear gate and come out with their hands on top of their heads," Barrabas told Lee as O'Toole and the others joined them at the captured personnel carrier.

The battlefield surgeon gave him a doubtful look. "They aren't going to buy it."

"Ask anyway."

She spoke in Russian to the troopers trapped in the BTR. They shouted something back at her.

"What did they say?"

"Something unkind about your mother..."

"I fix," Naazmomad said, hopping up on the rear corner of the BTR, unbolting an auxiliary gas tank from its rack. He opened the twenty-gallon drum and started pouring fuel over the roof and down into the vent-firing ports at the hinges.

The yelling from inside the personnel carrier got suddenly louder.

Naazmomad jumped onto the BTR's nose where its occupants could see him and pulled out a disposable lighter. He grinned as he prepared to roast the lot.

More yelling, this time in unison. The Soviets were all shouting the same thing.

"They'll do as we say," Lee said, translating.

The rear gate dropped a little, and AKs started flying out through the gap. The gate then lowered to the ground.

"Tell 'em to come out one at a time," Barrabas said.

The troopers did so, hands on their heads. As they came out, the SOBs stripped off the greatcoats, boots and earflap hats of the first eight. They tied all of them up with their own belts and left them sitting on hard ground in a line.

"You are foreign mercenaries! American fascists!" the driver said in passable English as he was hauled back to the BTR by the collar by Billy Two.

"You're about to join our cause," Barrabas told him. "If only briefly."

The Mongolian driver scowled at him.

"You're going to get us inside the fortress."

"Never!"

"You do have a choice," Barrabas told him. He indicated the other captives sitting helpless, trussed on the rocks. "You can stay here with them. Naazmomad, there, will be baby-sitting."

The guide paused in the honing of his skinning knife to beam over at the driver.

"I go with you," the man said flatly.

15

"Ram it again!" Barrabas ordered the captured driver.

Through the rear gate's slit windows the burning BTR still blocked their way out of the KZ.

The driver revved up and popped his vehicle into reverse. It lurched backward violently, slamming the hulk broadside. The collision sent the driver's passengers, the SOBs, sprawling. It nudged the destroyed BTR just far enough out of the way so they could back around it.

The collision did not budge the muzzle of Barrabas's AK from the side of the driver's neck.

"Nice work, Ivan," he said from the copilot's seat. "Now just keep it in reverse until you find a post where we can turn around. Take it slow and easy. It's starting to get dark out there."

The other mercenaries picked themselves up and resumed pulling on the borrowed Soviet outerwear, hats, boots and woolen long coats.

Nanos donned the garments with much grumbling and obvious disgust.

"What's the matter, Greek?" O'Toole said. "Want to send it to your tailor first?"

"Send it to be fumigated, you mean."

"Hey, you got nothing to worry about," Liam assured him. "Communism isn't catching. Right, Doc?"

Lee Hatton scowled. "Tell that to the mujahedeen, the Poles, the Hungarians, the Czechs, the East Germans, the..." She let her voice trail off.

The driver got the BTR turned the right way, its headlights illuminating slick planes of rock as they retraced the route to the fort.

"I bet ol' Naazmomad is having himself a time right now," Nanos said. "All those nice pink ears..."

"Maybe we shouldn't have left him alone with those guys?" Beck speculated.

"We aren't here to referee the Geneva Accords," Barrabas said. "We're here to pull off a dirty little job. I'll tell you one thing: whatever Naazmomad does or doesn't do to the prisoners we took, he had better be in the assigned spot when the time for a retreat comes or we're all going to be dead."

"Time for our first radio broadcast, Colonel?" Beck asked. "I got the antenna hooked up the way you wanted."

"Static?"

"Snowstorm quality," Beck said.

"Okay, Ivan," the white-haired man said to the driver, "tell them you are under attack. Say, 'We are under attack!' Tell them four times in exactly those words."

"And don't forget who understands Russian," Lee reminded him.

The Russian did as he was told. There was an urgency in his voice that could not be faked.

Beck shut off the transmitter's hand mike. Through the receiver speaker the fort was asking for a slow repeat of the message and further details. All they got for their trouble was more static.

"That ought to stir their curiosity," Liam said.

The BTR started up the long grade to the fort. The high stone walls of the garrison loomed above them, a bleak outpost atop a mountain without trees, shrubs or blade of grass. The klieg lights of the fortress made the slope of polished rock glisten wetly; they pinned the advancing BTR, tracking its slow, deliberate approach.

"Let's hope to hell they don't get too stirred up," Hayes said.

Barrabas's eyes narrowed. Driving so slowly under enemy guns made his skin crawl, but it had to be done. He shook off the unpleasant sensation. They had other much more important things to consider.

"Check your explosive packs," he told the others.

Each of the mercenaries had four C-4 bomb devices. They were two pounds of plastic explosive each, plus detonators and timers. A pair of the packs fitted easily into the slash pockets of the captured greatcoats.

When everyone had double-checked the sabotage gear, Barrabas said, "Let's sync watches. At the mark, I make it 8:39. Mark!"

The BTR swayed from side to side as it followed the tight turns of the switchbacks. They were right under the walls now, still moving in a pool of intense klieg light.

"Billy and Nanos," the colonel said, "get two explosive packs ready, one each. As we go through the gate, toss them out the firing ports on opposite sides. Set the timers to blow fifteen seconds after we pass through the entrance." He turned to Beck. "I think it's time to repeat the message again," he said.

Again the static-riddled, half-intelligible message was transmitted. The response from the fort this time was absolutely frantic. And with cause: three BTRs had gone out and only one was returning.

As the gates opened, Beck fully connected the antenna. The driver spoke as he had been coached.

"Mujahedeen! Mujahedeen! Thousands of them!" he cried. "Call an air strike! An air strike! They are coming! They are right behind me!"

It was a futile plea and that was how Barrabas wanted it. No way would Kabul dispatch gunships to fight a rebel night attack; the garrison was on its own. And every soldier inside the walls damn well knew it.

"Dump 'em," Barrabas said.

Billy Two and Nanos pushed explosive parcels out the BTR's rear firing ports.

As the personnel carrier drove into the compound, as the massive gates began to close, the night was ripped by a pair of thunderous explosions that shook the ground and spewed smoke and dirt high in the air. Rocks clanged against the roof and their BTR as it rolled across the compound. Through the radio, through the camp loudspeaker system, the garrison commander was screaming to his troops.

The panic was full-blown, soldiers running madly in all directions to get to battle stations. A heavy machine gun on the wall behind them opened fire, spearing the darkness with green tracers, shooting at nothing.

"Time to join the fun," Barrabas said, giving Hayes the sign to open the personnel carrier's rear gate.

Outside, two more heavy MGs on the wall started cutting loose at an invisible enemy.

"What about me?" the driver said.

Lee was ready to answer his question. She leaned forward and sank a hypodermic into his shoulder, injecting him with enough barbiturates to make him sleep soundly through the next day.

"Nighty-night," she said as he slumped against the driver's door.

"On the numbers now," Barrabas said. "We meet at the top of the north wall in eight minutes."

The mercenaries rushed out of the BTR and were instantly swept up in the chaos of a garrison "under attack."

Barrabas, Beck and Hayes ran in a ragged line past the barracks, skirting the unoccupied helicopter pad. They paused beside the twin hundred-thousand-gallon metal tanks, one water, the other diesel fuel. The entrance to the chemwar bunker was below ground level. Some twenty-five meters away a short flight of steps led down to a doorway.

Behind them another blast.

The barracks building's front wall blew out in a sheet of orange, a rolling wave of debris, wood, rock, glass skittered across the center of the compound.

"I'll go first," Barrabas said, trotting toward the steps.

Two Soviet privates guarded the door. They took halfhearted aim at Barrabas as he descended the stairs. They looked confused and frightened. Undoubtedly they were thinking about their skins and what it would feel like to lose them, inch by inch, to a mujahedeen blade.

"Open at once!" Barrabas snarled in what Lee had instructed him as appropriate Russian.

The ground shook from another blast, then another. Debris rained down into the stairwell.

The tall, grim-faced man shouted at the two privates and they caved in without protest, lowering their weapons. One of them turned and unlocked the padlock on the metal door. "Report to the main gate!" Barrabas ordered.

The voice of command was the same in any language.

The privates saluted and dashed up the steps.

Beck and Hayes came down a second after they had gone. The three mercenaries entered the dark bunker. Barrabas found the switch and turned on the lights. They found themselves in a low-ceilinged anteroom. Barrabas scanned the room quickly. They had to hurry. Once Billy Two blew the power supply generators, the place would be permanently dark. Around the walls were rows of coat hooks. Below them were empty shelves.

"A dressing room?" Hayes said.

"Looks like," Barrabas said.

Beck opened the door at the end of the room. "Come on, through here," he said.

They passed into a shower room. It was fully tiled with drains set in the floor. It reeked of chlorine and disinfectant.

"For decontamination," Beck told them. "A precautionary routine after handling chemwar materials. It also would be used in case of an accident.

The showers ended in another door. Beyond it was yet another dressing room. This one was lined with low metal benches. Along one wall on specially built racks hung olive green chemwar suits: fullhead masks with twin goggle-eyed view ports, corrugated hoses trailing from the nose and mouth area, connected to rebreather bags. There were also long butyl rubber overcoats, gauntlets, pants and boots.

The second dressing room ended in a pair of doors. They were made of heavy-gauge steel and each had a knurled stainless steel handle. Stenciled boldly across the front was a warning in Russian. In the two doors there were three separate places for a key to fit into a lock. A different key for each aperture. There were no keys in sight.

"Damn!" Beck groaned as he wrenched the handles apart with all his strength. They moved a fraction of an inch down and no more.

The chemwar materials vault was locked.

Barrabas and Hayes just stared at the doors.

That the Soviets would take such extraordinary precautions inside a secure fort had seemed only a remote possibility back in Peshawar.

"Colonel," Beck said, "we're out of luck. No way can we get to the stockpile without blowing this door off its hinges. If we do that . . ."

"If we do that," Hayes finished for him, "the Russians are sure as hell going to know someone has been in here, fooling around with their secret weapon. They're going to check over every inch of the place before they even think about trying to move the gas."

Barrabas checked his watch. "Not to mention the fact that we don't have time to plant charges on the doors, get out, blow them open, get back in here and set fresh charges under the stockpile. The lights are going to go out in this place in a little less than two minutes."

"That means this mission is a total, flat-out bust," Hayes said grimly.

"All those saddle sores for nothing," Beck added, shaking his head.

The tendons in Barrabas's jaws flexed as he ground his teeth. He did not like being shut out. Especially so close to the goal. He still had two minutes to think it all through, to find another way, and he was determined to use every second at his disposal.

Barrabas turned, surveying, glaring at the contents of the room, and suddenly froze. A grin spread over his face. "I think I know how we can salvage the mission," he said.

LEE HATTON FELT LOST in her stolen overcoat. It was huge, the hem dragging in the dirt behind her. The boots were loose, too, the hat too big. Some disguise, she thought as she trotted to the right of the main gate. The Soviets charging around her were too nervous to notice the poor fit. She stopped in front of a parked BTR, discreetly took an explosive parcel from her coat pocket, set the timer for half a minute, then hurried on.

The bomb exploded just as she reached one of the flights of stone stairs leading up to the catwalk around the top of the perimeter wall. She crouched and cowered as metal bits whined off the wall.

Behind her was the BTR service and storage area. A partially roofed-over section of the fort's interior. Dismantled diesel engines sat on tables, hung from chain hoists. She set a timer for another thirty seconds and flipped the bomb onto the stone flagging. It skidded under a workbench.

As she hurried up the steps she saw a figure atop the wall above her. It was a man in a coat like hers, with an AK like hers. He was staring at her.

Then the shop blew.

Its roof ruptured up and out, individual sheets of corrugated tin flying through the air like giant playing cards, fire sweeping through the whole service area.

Lee reached the catwalk and turned left, running.

The man shouted for her to stop.

She did not.

He chased her and in Russian he shouted again. "Stop or I'll shoot!"

Lee stopped.

BILLY TWO CHUCKED a ticking plastic bomb through an open window of the barracks on the run. He barely got around the corner of the building before it went off. The blast knocked him flat on his backside.

Over his shoulder, the front roof of the barracks collapsed as its load-bearing wall was blown out. Flames leaped up from the ragged gash in the roof.

Before he could get up himself, a Soviet soldier grabbed his hand and helped him to his feet. The man didn't hang around to be thanked, which was just as well because Starfoot only knew how to swear in Russian.

"Cut it too damn fine," he told himself as he reached into his pocket and took out another bomb.

Men in uniform were running all around him, but none paid him any mind. He set the timer for two minutes and jogged for the power supply building. It was a stone hut that housed the fort's generators. He tried the door. It was unlocked.

Inside, the noise of generators was deafening. Billy Two slipped the explosives beneath a metal housing and made a quick exit.

He looked up at the big kliegs ringing the inside of the perimeter wall. They turned night into day in the enclosure. Their opposite numbers, aimed downslope, did the same for the mountainside. But not for long.

Billy broke into a run, heading for the huge water and diesel storage tanks. He could see Nanos waiting for him in the shadows of the fuel reservoir. The two of them were going to turn the lights back on again.

With diesel.

O'TOOLE STUCK THE BARREL of his AK over the top of the perimeter wall, aimed at nothing in particular and ripped off a brisk 10-round, full-auto burst. The 7.62 mm x 39 empties clattered to the stone pavings at his feet. The ComBloc troopers on either side of him did the same, firing wildly into the fringe of blackness beyond the range of the kliegs, at the bottom of the mountainside.

All along the catwalk the cream of Russian manhood unloaded 30-round magazines as if they were going out of style.

Liam glared sidelong at the panic-stricken young men. It was not a pretty sight for an Army officer, even an ex-officer, to behold. O'Toole had always considered the Soviet soldier to be better trained, better disciplined, better commanded than their performance tonight indicated. His previous experience was, however, against Spetsnaz, Soviet Special Forces. The kids beside him on the wall were not handpicked volunteers; they were draftees. Who had drawn shit duty.

Maybe they had fought mujahedeen hand to hand before? Maybe they had seen a few of their countrymen without their birthday suits? Or with cheeks stuffed full of their own severed genitalia? Whatever the reason, the boys with the red stars on their hats were out of control.

The barracks directly behind and below him exploded. Liam turned in time to see a ball of flame erupt from under the ripped roof. He put his AK on his shoulder and hurried down the catwalk. When he came to the stone tower, he slowed down.

Originally, the Mogul defenders of the fort had poured boiling oil and burning pitch down on attackers from the three elliptical towers. It was state of the art in the sixteenth century. Now the towers sported pairs of 12.7 mm antiaircraft guns, which jutted from armored, motorized turrets and delivered an infinitely more deadly rain.

Liam adjusted the timers on two packs of C-4 and placed them both at the back of the right-hand gun turret. It was the only one that counted.

LEE HATTON TURNED and faced her accuser. From a distance of two meters the Russian noncom recognized her as a woman at once. There were no women in the garrison. He was astonished, but not so astonished that he let his point of aim shift from her chest.

"Put down your gun," he said.

Lee started to obey, the expression on her pretty face resigned, defeated. It was a ruse. As she lowered the rifle, she moved forward. The noncom reached for the gun with one hand, covering her with the other. Lee slipped aside, thrusting the muzzle of the AK between the man's knees as he lunged, tripping him up. She used the buttstock like a lever, knocking him to the side. His back slammed against the iron railing that rimmed the inside of the catwalk.

Before he could regain his balance, Lee shouldered him over.

He fell headfirst thirty meters to the stones below, screaming all the way.

Then the power station exploded, and all the electric lights in the place winked out. The only illumination was from the fires burning below. In the ghastly shifting light nobody paid any attention to the crumpled body on the flags.

Lee sprinted to the stone tower just above and past the BTR service area and set two bombs behind the left-hand MG turret. With the machine guns on the inside of both towers knocked out, the SOBs' escape route to the summit was clear, except for possible assault-rifle fire.

BARRABAS DREW HIS SLIM BLACK STILETTO from its wrist sheath and picked up the corrugated hose of one of the chemwar suit's rebreather units. He bent the flexible hose in a U, then carefully sliced the stretch rubber on the outside of the bend with the fine point of the blade. When he let the hose snap back, the slit he had made was invisible.

Both Beck and Hayes got the picture without further explanation. They pulled out their own daggers and hurriedly set to work on the remaining protective suits.

"HEY, WE'RE SUPPOSED TO BLOW UP THE FUEL," Nanos said to his Indian friend. "Why are you messing around with the goddam water tank?"

"Ever take science in school?" Billy Two said as he attached a two-pound chunk of plastic explosive to the side of the water reservoir.

"Sure, we had to."

"Hard science. Not sex ed."

"Sex ed wasn't easy where I went to school. For the final we had both a written and an oral exam."

"And how many times did you fail the oral?"

"Hey, could I help it if as a youngster I was tongue-tied?"

"Look, Alex, it's simple. Diesel floats on water. The two substances won't mix. If we blow up the water tank first, then the fuel, the diesel will ride the wave of water, spread further and burn more area. Got it?"

"Did you think that up yourself?"

"Why?"

"Because it sounds like Beck talking to me."

"Beck who?"

"Right, Mr. Science," Nanos said, planting his charges at the base of the fuel tank.

They were halfway up the steps to the catwalk behind the chemwar bunker when the power station exploded and the lights went out. When the rolling boom faded, all the shooting stopped. The yelling continued. Then the shooting started up again. The atheist invaders were convinced they were about to be overrun by crazed natives.

Billy and Nanos joined the others at the now dark klieg lights on the catwalk. A rappeling line had already been attached to the base of the lights. It trailed down the outside of the wall. Gunther was already on the ground below and Lee was descending rapidly.

"How'd it go?" Nanos asked Barrabas. "Did you booby-trap the arsenal?"

"We couldn't get to the arsenal, so we had to improvise."

"Improvise?"

Hayes butted in. "All their antichemical warfare suits have holes in them."

"Real tiny holes?" Billy asked

"Real tiny holes," Hayes answered, taking hold of the rope in gloved hands and starting his descent.

Then the two tanks exploded.

A split second apart.

Time enough for a five-foot-high wave of water to sweep through the stone courtyard. The second blast was even more spectacular. The heat from the detonating plastic explosive ignited the fumes trapped in the top of the tank. A ball of orange and red twice as high as the fort's walls howled into the sky.

"Holy shit!" Alex cried.

Inside the courtyard a burning lake of fuel engulfed running men. Fire was everywhere at once, sucking down a raging wind to feed itself. The only soldiers to survive the flames were the ones atop the wall. They looked on, helpless, while their comrades died. Then two MG turrets exploded. Steel-plate shrapnel screamed through the air. And not even the wall was safe.

Barrabas was the last man to take hold of the rope. As he did, he looked at the madly leaping flames and smiled. The SOBs had added considerably to the legend of the mujahedeen this night. The destruction of the garrison by apparently invisible foes would haunt the dreams of the Soviet invaders for years to come. And with any luck, the next combat test of Soman II would be its last.

He rappeled down the wall and joined the others. They raced single file in darkness up the hill to the freestanding spires on the summit. Waiting on a narrow trail just below was Naazmomad. He had the horses with him.

16

The MI-24 gunship circled the Mogul fortress three times, then plummeted like a runaway elevator car to the courtyard's helicopter pad.

With sinking heart, as well as sinking stomach, Dr. Hermann Ulm watched the ancient fort rush up at him. If anything, early reports from the scene of the attack had downplayed the extent of the damage. Within the defensive perimeter wall, not a single Soviet structure remained standing. All was rubble, fire-blackened rubble. Indeed, it was impossible to tell for certain where the buildings had been. The debris was strewn, by explosion and the burst water tank, in scattered unrecognizable heaps. Here and there gutted hulks of personnel carriers lay overturned. Dirty black water. Charred bodies lay facedown in it. Small teams of Soviet soldiers with white handkerchiefs tied over their noses were counting corpses and covering them with sheets of black plastic.

As the gunship landed, its rotor wind whipped water, ash and debris. It also blew the coverings off a half dozen Russian dead. Four more Hinds followed the lead ship down.

Major Vlad Shirkov shut off the gunship's engine. As he unbuckled his seat harness he turned to Ulm, pale faced, white knuckled in the copilot's chair. "So much for your secret weapon," he said with gleeful malice. "It looks like the war in Afghanistan may just drag on a little while longer, doesn't it, Professor?"

Ulm said nothing. A recitation of his feeble hopes for the survival of the Soman II material would have been pathetic and only increased the major's pleasure. He unlocked his seat harness and got out of the helicopter. The stench of burned wood, rubber and flesh nearly made him gag. The garrison's commanding officer was there to meet him.

"A disaster," the CO said, waving a hand at the ruin. His eyes had a haunted look, his smile was brittle. "All I can say is that it was a miracle we were able to turn back the rebel attack, that we didn't lose the fort altogether."

"So it would appear," Major Shirkov said as he rounded the nose of the gunship. "What did they hit you with? A Howitzer? Mortars?"

"We are still unsure."

"Whatever they used," Shirkov said, looking around, "they used to maximum advantage."

"You say you weren't actually overrun?" Ulm asked.

The CO shook his head.

"How close did they get?" Shirkov said.

"We have no way of telling," the commander told them. "The generators were hit shortly after the attack began. All the floodlights went out. We were blind firing most of the night."

"How many dead rebels did you recover this morning?" the major asked.

The CO's brittle smile got broader and more forced. "That is the truly unbelievable part. This morning, when we searched the slopes, we found no bodies. The mujahedeen must have recovered all their dead during the night."

"And under fire," Shirkov said doubtfully. "I never knew them to be so fastidious."

"They did it to scare us," the garrison commander went on. "To make us think none of them were harmed, while we took heavy losses."

"How heavy?"

"Eighty-five percent."

Ulm's impatience with the formality of official condolence and the predictability of military curiosity got the better of him. He didn't give a damn how many Russian draftees the rebels chewed up as long as the contents of his precious underground bunker remained undisturbed.

"Can we have a look at the chemical-weapons storage facility?" he asked the CO.

"Yes, of course," the man said, leading the way through the shallow lake that had formed in the lowest portion of the courtyard. The bunker was at the high end of the interior and as such, out of the four inches of ash-stained standing water.

They walked down the stairs to the bunker door.

As the CO unlocked the lock, Shirkov said, "You are sure that the rebels did not climb the outer wall and get in after the lights went out?"

"If they had," the commander said, "then they would be as dead as the troopers under the tarps and we would have found their corpses by now. The fuel tank exploded shortly after the power failed. Everyone in the courtyard was burned to death. The fuel fire burned itself out after daybreak. No one got in before the fire. And after the fire no one got out."

When the CO opened the door, they could all see a broad puddle of water on the floor. It had seeped in under the door. The garrison commander turned on the bunker's interior lights. They flickered, then held. "We've got an auxiliary generator going," he told them as they stepped through the puddle.

"If anyone had come in after the attack," Ulm said, pointing at the dry section of floor, "there would be wet footprints deeper in the bunker."

"Let's see the storage vault," Shirkov said coldly.

The trio walked through the shower room and into the area where the protective suits were stored. The major and the professor only gave the neatly hanging suits the briefest of glances before proceeding to the vault's double doors.

"No sign of tampering," Ulm said, peering at the locks and the hinges.

Shirkov examined the doors and said nothing.

The CO opened the locks, then the doors. Inside, stacked in waist-high pyramids, were chemwar rockets and warheads.

"Wonderful!" Ulm exclaimed. "The bunker survived the fire completely intact. There is no reason why we can't continue the combat mission as planned."

Shirkov grunted.

Ulm beamed. He was no longer at the mercy of bureaucrats and yes-men. He had the green light to change the world. He was determined to seize the opportunity by the throat. To seize all opportunities that presented themselves to him.

In his most irritating, most pompous tone, he addressed the CO, but spoke solely for the major's benefit. "Soon you won't have to worry about fighting these rebels, Commander. If my Soman II performs half as well as expected, in less than a month it will have killed them all, rendered their sanctuaries useless and put you out of a job."

Major Shirkov about-faced and stormed out of the bunker.

"Can we begin loading the warheads at once?" Ulm asked the CO. There was a decided lilt to his voice.

17

Tajik Bula pretended to be asleep on his thin, woven reed mat. All around him on the cave floor, the assembled freedom fighters of Allah were not faking. They snored, they snorted, they muttered aloud, expounding great truths in dream conversations. Outside the cave it was almost midday; inside it was twilight. The rebels were not lazy; they slept by day and did their fighting at night. The better to harass the much-hated atheist invaders whose work and war schedules were not nearly so flexible.

Under Tajik's head, wrapped up in his quilted coat, was the Soviet homing device. At his right hand was the black gun he had sold his family and his village for.

A great lump rose in young Bula's throat. He wanted to wake Aziz, who slept beside him. To confess everything. He even reached out once, but drew back his hand before he made contact. What was the point, after all, he asked himself countless times. To confess his crime was to die. Not to fulfill his mission for Khad was to die. He would have confessed, anyway, regardless of the consequences, but he didn't want Aziz to think badly of him. He had done much inadvertent evil in order to impress others with his "heroism," Aziz in particular. Now that he had made that impression, he could not bear to see it, too, destroyed. Even if it meant that all the soldiers of Allah would be killed.

Whose fault was it that he was weak? Allah had made him. Therefore it was Allah's fault! And having made him, Allah should have known better than to tempt him, should have known he would fail.

Tajik rolled over on his sleeping mat. He looked at the watch on the wrist of a snoring mujahedeen. It was a quarter past noon, time to do the thing. The gunship raid was scheduled for 1:00 P.M., when the sun would be hard in the eyes of the rebels manning the mountaintop antiaircraft positions. It was also the hour of the day when most of the guerrillas would be in one place, sleeping soundly.

Quietly the skinny boy rose from the ground. He picked up the bundle of his coat and his black gun. Carefully he stepped over the curled-up body of Aziz, then he moved around the other reclining bodies on the cave floor.

Not everyone was asleep. A group of men seated around a teakettle looked up when he passed. They smiled. He smiled. They did not question him. He was free to come and go as he pleased. It pleased him now to go, forever.

The daylight blinded Tajik when he stepped out from the cave entrance. He slid his bundled coat under his right arm and rubbed his eyes with his knuckles. The view was magnificent. A crescent of snowcapped mountain peaks, jagged and shining, trailed pennant-wisps of clouds across a brilliant blue sky. The line of mountains went on and on, one behind the other for as far as he could see.

To look down was to grow weak in the knees. The valley some three thousand meters below was partially obscured by a bank of low clouds. The path leading to the mujahedeen cave was hardly a path at all. If someone didn't know how to read the markers, he would never reach it. And never survive the attempt.

Tajik moved to the edge of the cave's entrance, looked around to see if anyone was watching, then set down his AK. He started climbing up the side of the mountain and stopped after advancing only a few meters. He took the device from his coat, pulled out the antenna to full length and turned on the switch. The red light came on, signaling that the device was operational. He put the little black box down in a crevice behind a rock. Satisfied that it was well hidden, he looked below him. Still seeing no one, he climbed down.

It was with a terrible sadness that he returned to the cave entrance to retrieve his gun. He could not plead ignorance this time. He knew the exact nature of his crime. He knew precisely the sort of death the true heroes would meet. Death by poison gas.

"May Allah forgive me," he said aloud, then he shouldered his AK and started down the trail, down the mountain, away from the doomed mujahedeen.

AZIZ WAS NOT ASLEEP, EITHER. He had slept a little since the meeting in Kabul between Tajik and the older boy. He was troubled by many things. The shock over the loss of his mother, father, brothers and sisters had faded and with it the numbness that had blunted his grief. No such barrier existed now. His sorrow was a constant ache at the center of his heart. He had begun to dream about his dead family, too. And in his dreams he saw them dying. And they saw him. They begged him to avenge their murders. And in his dream, as in real life, he could not answer back that he was only a boy.

He was troubled by Tajik, as well. The other boy hardly talked anymore. And when he did, sometimes his eyes would suddenly fill with tears, for no apparent reason. Whenever Aziz tried to get him to speak about the "debt" he owed his half-cousin, he would change the subject or excuse himself and walk away. Aziz had begun to think that Tajik's problem with Khwaja revolved around the black gun. After seeing young Bula in combat, he had serious doubts about the boy's ability to kill an armed Soviet soldier with a rock and a knife. And if that wasn't how Tajik got the gun, then how had he?

The gun had appeared after a trip to Kabul. And on that same trip to Kabul Tajik had incurred a large debt to his half-cousin. It was logical, then, that the debt was because of the black gun, that Tajik had received the weapon from Khwaja, promising to pay for it at some future date. The difficulty with this hypothesis was in the size of the debt. It was hard to believe that someone who seemed as sharp as Khwaja would lend a farm boy two thousand dollars U.S. It was an amount he could never repay. The only possible answer seemed to be that repayment was not to be in kind. Aziz could not imagine a service Tajik could provide the older boy that would be worth so much money.

It was with these thoughts that Aziz wrestled as he lay in fetal position on his sleeping mat. His eyes were closed when the shadow of Tajik passed over him. He felt the movement of air and looked up.

The other boy was stealthily slipping out of the sleeping area, black gun in hand.

Aziz waited until Tajik passed through the gap in the ragged makeshift blanket curtain that separated the cave's mass bedroom from the eating, storage and meeting sections, then he, too, rose and followed.

He hung back in the darkness along the cave wall as Tajik stepped out into the sunlight. When the boy set down his black gun and began to climb, Aziz hurried to the edge of the cave's broad entrance.

Aziz did not show himself. He peered around the arch, then ducked back. Tajik was clinging to the almost vertical rock face ten meters above him and a few meters to the left. Aziz peeked again. The other boy was taking something out of his rolled-up coat and carefully placing it in a crack. Aziz pulled back just as Tajik turned to look down. Then he heard some bits of rock falling and he knew the other boy was climbing down. Aziz stepped back into the shadows of the entrance.

When Tajik retrieved his black gun, he stared into the dim cave for a long moment. Aziz thought he had been discovered. But then young Bula said something. Not Aziz's name. Tajik asked God to forgive him. Then he set off down the path.

Aziz waited until the boy was out of sight, then scrambled up the front of the cliff. He reached into the crevice and took out the thing Tajik had hidden. A black plastic box with a thin silver antenna and a red light. His heart thudded as he turned it over and saw the writing on the back.

The writing was in Russian.

18

Ahmad Yar slowly twisted a tendril of gray beard around his callused index finger as, stone faced, he watched the members of his war council angrily debate. The argument was over provisions and deployment of men. That there was an argument at all, that the council pointedly ignored his presence revealed the true nature of the crisis.

A crisis in confidence.

The eyes of the leader of the Jamiat-I-Islamis, yellow-brown and hard as gemstone, showed no reaction to the words being said. Inside, however, Ahmad Yar seethed with rage.

His authority as headman was being openly, if not directly, challenged.

Not by one of his captains.

By all of them.

This was his reward for leading the rebels to so many glorious victories against the invaders? It was a pill too bitter for Ahmad Yar to swallow.

The trouble had begun immediately after the incident with the foreign mercenaries. That he had capitulated to their strength, ordered a disgraceful retreat, allowed valuable weapons and ammunition to slip through the hands of his people had infuriated the war council.

It wasn't just material, either.

The escape of the infidel woman who had killed one of their own, an escape from the sword of justice, had not helped matters at all. Justice aside, in a jihad, a holy war, there were not many opportunities to engage in the normal sexual release of men in combat. Rape. Only very rarely did a suitable female, that is, one not of the faith, wander into range.

Ahmad Yar had lost much face to the white-haired man. He gnashed his teeth as he considered his alternative. To challenge the captains now, to bluff them down without a cause to rally behind, was to invite real and permanent disaster. If he tried and the war council turned their backs on him, he would never be able to recover his authority.

He would be an outcast.

The headman could stand to listen to the endless bickering no longer. "You sound like a group of old women!" he snarled, rising from the rock on which he sat. "You make me sick."

With that he turned his back on them.

He walked away. There was only silence behind him. Let them consider, he thought, what it would be like to go into battle without an experienced leader. Let them consider the number of their dead.

Ahmad Yar walked to the edge of a cliff. Below him was the dry, barren valley of the Jamiat. It was his place. It was Allah's place. He knelt and prayed for guidance from Allah.

The stones hurt his knees but he did not rise.

He would not rise until he had received an answer.

Some twenty minutes later Allah spoke to him.

The message came through the vessel of a rebel scout who rushed up breathless with excitement. The scout said, "Ahmad Yar, they are back!"

Yar opened his eyes and raised his forehead from the earth. "Who are back?"

"The foreigners! They ride up the valley from the west."

Ahmad Yar stood, his eyes alight with glee. Allah had chosen to answer his prayers. Ahmad Yar now had his rallying point. He could reclaim the leadership of his fighters. And he would have revenge.

"Gather the men!" he ordered the scout. Then he strode back to the council to assert his power.

THE HORSE UNDER NILE BARRABAS moved no faster than it had on the journey out, but somehow the trip seemed shorter. Perhaps because he remembered parts of the terrain, distances between points, he could measure their progress. Also he could enjoy the trek and the scenery without worrying about the outcome of the mission.

For better or worse, the mission was over.

In front of him, Naazmomad broke trail. Behind him, the other SOBs were strung out in a ragged line. He could hear them joking and jiving one another.

"So what's the first thing you're going to do when you get back to civilization?" Beck was asking Liam.

O'Toole smiled. His face was dark with grime and soot and he had a five-day growth of red beard. "Before or after I take a shower in carbolic acid?"

"After, please."

"I'm going to make love to a quart of Bushmill's and pass out cold."

"How nice for you both," Dr. Lee said.

"Me," Gunther butted in, "I'm going to eat some decent food for a change."

Nanos made a face at Billy Two. "What does a Dutchman mean by 'decent food'?"

"Raw herring?" the Indian ventured.

"The food of the gods," Gunther said.

"Hey, you guys, there's nothing wrong with herring," Beck told them.

"Right," the Greek said. "But the people who fancy it for breakfast are another story. Have you ever awakened to a prune Danish, orange juice and a big plate of pickled fish?''

"No," Beck admitted, "but this girl I met in Vancouver once . . ."

As the conversation took off on a further bizarre tangent, Barrabas's mind began to wander. He had heard Beck's tale of the mysterious girl in the Canadian hotel room before. He knew she had removed a wig, false eyelashes, an industrial strength girdle and both upper and lower sets of teeth before sliding into bed with the computer whiz. He remembered the story's punch line, if only vaguely. Something about getting what you paid for. In the colonel's opinion, it was all just dumb enough to have really happened the way Beck claimed.

The white-haired man had some serious misgivings about the mission they had just completed. His doubts were not about whether the SOBs had done the best job they could under the circumstances. No battle plan was foolproof. Especially with limited intel resources, limited personnel and equipment. There were too many uncontrollable variables when operating behind enemy lines; there was no way to account for them all. The hit-and-run jobs dealt out to the Soldiers of Barrabas always relied heavily on last-second improvisation. The doubts that nagged him on the way out of Afghanistan were over the correctness of one such improvised choice: the choice he had made in the Russian chemwar bunker.

There was always a chance that the protective gear would be tested thoroughly before it was used again. The suits were routinely inflated with air and checked for leaks. The corrugated hose, however, was much more difficult to test. It had to be disconnected from the rebreather unit and checked separately. Because the hose was made of much thicker rubber, maintenance checks were required less frequently than for the main suit.

There was one consolation. If the trick did work, they would find out in short order. The self-destruction of an entire Soviet chemwar unit was not the kind of news the mujahedeen would keep to themselves.

Barrabas's attention returned to the here and now as Naazmomad led the group down into a canyon. On either side of the sandy wash, gray rock walls loomed straight up. They had been carved in sweeping curves by the river, now dry, as it meandered through the bedrock.

The SOBs stopped talking when they descended into the cut. Their voices would have otherwise echoed and carried in the enclosed space, and they all knew they were passing again through the territory controlled by the Jamiat-I-Islamis. The only sounds in the canyon were of horses' hooves crunching sand and the animals' breathing as they plodded along.

The farther they traveled, the higher the bracketing walls became. Barrabas got a strange feeling as the walls grew taller. A kind of chill that had nothing to do with temperature. He scanned the rounded ridge tops, squinting into the sun's glare.

O'Toole rode up alongside him. "You, too, Colonel?"

Barrabas nodded. "We'd better start looking for a good place to make a stand. If we wait much longer, the choice will no longer be ours." He called softly to the guide.

Naazmomad turned on his saddle and looked back.

As he did so, gunfire rained down on them from above and from a rockfall across the canyon bottom about forty meters away. It was instant chaos. Steel-cored slugs skipped off rocks, shattered, ricocheted. The horses reared and bucked, terrified by the noise.

Naazmomad grimaced in pain as a ComBloc round caught him low in the back. The impact slammed him sideways. Unable to keep his seat, he toppled from the horse.

"Take cover!" Barrabas yelled, dismounting and running to help the fallen man. He and Liam pulled the guide to the relative safety of a cleft between some rocks, and all the while bullets screamed overhead.

They weren't the only thing screaming.

One of the horses had been hit and was down. It shrieked as it thrashed and kicked on its side in the sand.

A single rifle shot, close at hand, put a merciful end to its suffering.

The fire aimed at the mercenaries dwindled, then dropped to nothing.

"Who's hurt?" Barrabas shouted to the others down the line of outcrops.

"No one," Lee answered after a moment.

"Doc, get over here," the colonel said. "Naazmomad's been shot."

Movement by the doctor brought on a fresh rain of bullets from above. She made it without a scratch, however.

When she reached Naazmomad, the Afghan guide already had a stick wedged between his clenched teeth and was gnawing the hell out of it.

"Jesus," Lee said, as she dropped the back of his trousers to examine the wound.

Liam looked, too. He put a hand on Naazmomad's shoulder. "A few inches lower and you'd have had a new..."

"You're going to be okay," Lee told the man. "It's just a flesh wound. The bullet passed cleanly through the meat of your buttocks."

"Going to be kind of hard to ride out of here, though," O'Toole said.

"Unless wc do something quick, none of us is going to ride out," Barrabas said. "All of you, move in closer."

The SOBs did as they were ordered.

"Alex, Starfoot," Barrabas said, "you two take the guys ahead of us. They've got to be cleared out, driven back before we can move."

"Right," the Indian said, crawling off with Nanos in tow.

"The rest of us will spread out and try to pick off as many as we can from the ridges above. We have no idea how many of them there are, so don't waste ammunition. Use single shots only, unless they decide to charge us."

As the SOBs slipped apart, the fusilade resumed.

Barrabas squinted up as more 7.62 mm Russian bullets pounded down all around him. It was asking for a slug between the eyes—not an easy thing to do, even if your life depended on it. He picked out a single muzzle-flash on a ledge high on the wall, snugged into his AK sling and aimed up through the weapon's iron sights.

The target was a pinpoint.

A head and shoulders more than seventy-five meters away.

The colonel slowly exhaled and squeezed the trigger. Once. The AK bucked into his shoulder and he rode the recoil wave back on target. He squeezed again. And again. The third shot was a charm.

First the Afghan's AK tumbled away from the ledge, clattering against the stone face, then the Afghan himself freefell, somersaulting over and over until he crashed on his back on a broad round rock. After he hit he did not move.

More single shots rang out from down the line of mercenaries.

They were answered by auto-fire from above.

"A double!" Liam shouted as a pair of dark forms plummeted to the canyon wash.

Fresh casualties did not decrease the enemy rate of fire.

Deeper in the canyon, Nanos and Billy Two crept to within twenty meters of the rockfall before they were pinned by steady, accurate fire.

"What now?" Nanos said.

"You're going back."

"Holy shit, do you really mean it? You'd send me back and face those crazy bastards all by yourself? Man, you are a buddy and a half!"

Billy Two smirked at him. "I'm sending you back to get the last LAW, musclehead."

"Oh."

The Indian shouldered his AK and sighted on the rockfall as the Greek crawled away. "And hurry!" he said out of the corner of his mouth.

By the time Nanos retraced the route between boulders and rejoined Barrabas and the others, the shooting from above had stopped. As had the shooting from below.

"They're not giving us any targets," Liam complained.

"Billy wants the last LAW," Nanos said.

The colonel gave him the go-ahead to take it. As Nanos started to drag himself back through the furrow he had worn in the sand, a gruff voice boomed down at them from above.

"Surrender!" it said. "Surrender or die!"

"It's that Yar guy," Lee said. "I recognize his voice."

"Me too," Barrabas said.

"What are we gonna do, Colonel?" Liam asked.

Barrabas cupped his hands to his mouth and shouted up. "What are your terms?"

"Give us all your weapons, all your ammunition and the woman and we will let you live."

"He's got to be kidding!" Liam exclaimed. "If we give up our guns, they'll slaughter us all for the practice."

"Everybody!" Barrabas said. "Count your bullets. Do it quick!"

The SOBs removed the magazines from their assault rifles, checked the cartridges and then tallied the remaining full clips they each had.

O'Toole passed on the bad news to the colonel. "Two and a half full mags apiece," he said. "The mules have the rest of the ammo strapped to their backs. And the mules went thataway." He indicated the direction they had come from.

"Not enough ammo to hold off a siege," Barrabas said. "If they want to they can just wait us out."

The voice from above boomed again. "The guns! The bullets! The woman! What is your answer?"

The SOBs exchanged grimaces.

"See if he'll just take the woman," Hayes suggested with a wink.

19

Aziz did not know what to do.

He did not recognize the device he held in his hand. He did not know what its purpose was.

Nor did he have a clue to the significance of the little red light that burned at one end of the box. Nor to the on-off button below it. He could not be sure whether pushing the button would, as logic dictated, turn the thing off or, if it was a bomb of some kind, cause it to instantly detonate.

What he did know was that the device was of Soviet manufacture and that his friend Tajik had taken some trouble to plant it close to the cave mouth and well out of sight. He also knew that Tajik hadn't wanted to wait around to see the results. Aziz deduced, therefore, that whatever the black box was meant to do, it was meant to do for the atheist invaders. And against the mujahedeen.

He took care not to push the button and made no attempt to close the extended antenna. He climbed down from the ledge, carrying the black box in one hand.

Once he had descended the cliff side and was back at the cave entrance again, he wondered if he should return to the sleeping area for his battered Enfield, the rifle he had inherited from the mujahedeen Tajik had killed by accident during the Kabul raid. He decided against going back for several reasons. He was afraid he would lose Tajik if he delayed pursuit any longer. The other boy was already well out of sight. Also, if the device was dangerous, as he believed it was, he did not want to take it inside the cave with him. He didn't want to leave it outside, either, for fear that it would do whatever it was meant to do before he could return and remove it.

His choices were, in fact, limited to one. He had to go after Tajik and take the device with him. He had a vague plan to confront the other boy with the black box and demand an explanation. But first he had to catch him.

The device in hand, Aziz started down the mountain.

As he walked, things began to fall into place; the facts contrasted with the lies started to make sense. Whether the debt Tajik owed his cousin was purely monetary or had something to do with the black gun, its repayment was connected to the planting of the device. It had to be. Where else could Tajik have gotten something like it? Who else did either of the boys know who could possibly have provided it? And when else could Tajik have had the opportunity to pick it up? Aziz had been with him almost constantly since the gas attack on their village. Aziz was positive Tajik hadn't had the device then. The other boy had only really been alone once, the night of the Kabul raid, the night he'd met Khwaja.

Aziz considered the cousin in a new light, as a provider of electronic gear of Russian manufacture to young Afghan boys. This Khwaja seemed to have no job, yet he was well-dressed and had an apartment of his own and plenty of spending money. The first thought that came to Aziz's mind after making the Soviet connection was Khad, the Afghan Secret Police. Stories about Khad using teenagers to gather information on the rebels, to sabotage the cause of the soldiers of Islam, had been around since the invasion began.

He looked at the black box in his hand. If Khad had caused it to be placed at the entrance to the mujahedeen cave, it was definitely something to be rid of, bomb or not. Something to be rid of quickly. He drew back his arm, preparing to hurl the thing out into space, but stopped. An explosion on the mountainside could start an avalanche and kill innocent people below. He had to find a safe place to dispose of the device, somewhere it could do no harm, no matter what its purpose.

Aziz had the answer.

There was another cave a good five hundred meters lower down on the trail. It wasn't used by the rebels for anything because it didn't go deep enough into the rock. Aziz picked up the pace of his walking, all the while keeping a lookout for Tajik ahead of him.

He did not see the other boy before he reached the second cave. Its entrance was easily as large as the main cave above, formed out of concentric rings of rock worn away by some natural process. Aziz stepped into the coolness and damp of the dark interior. The cave roof slanted down at a steep angle after three or four meters and the walls made a slight bend to the left, then dead-ended in a sheer rock face. Someone had once taken shelter there from a storm. The charred remains of an old fire lay scattered on the sandy floor.

Aziz carefully set the device against the back wall, then hurried out. He would move much faster now. He would catch Tajik and make him tell all.

TAJIK HAD NO IDEA he was being followed.

He did not dawdle, however. His worry was that he wouldn't get far enough away from the scene of the gunship attack, that he, too, would be killed by the gas.

As he picked his way across a long slide of loose, small stones, he searched the slope ahead for a sign of the trail. From some angles the trail markers were almost impossible to see and it was easy to get off on a false path.

He located a marker below him, then slid down the pile of rock to its level. Back on the right trail, he started to make his plans. He had put off doing any thinking about the future, because he hadn't decided what he was going to do about the homing device until the last minute.

Tajik knew if he returned to Kabul, he could sell the black gun for at least fifteen hundred dollars U.S. He had no attachment to the weapon; it had been nothing but trouble to him. With the money in hand, he could leave the country. He could go to Pakistan and start over there.

Or he could stay in Kabul and report back to Khwaja.

Having done the difficult and dangerous job he had been asked to do, there had to be some further reward for him. Or maybe more work in the same line. He could get some nice clothes, a big gold watch and an apartment of his own.

It was certainly something to think about.

Tajik wished to keep his options open. After all, he was only fourteen. He had his whole life ahead of him.

20

Major Vlad Shirkov squeezed his throat mike and gave the gunship crew the order to don protective head and breathing gear.

In the copilot's seat, Hermann Ulm had already pulled the chemically impervious butyl hood over his head. Through the rebreather unit, air had a sharp, sterile, rubber smell that he found comforting, if not pleasant.

On both flanks of the lead helicopter, stretched out in wedge formation, the twenty-ship attack force overflew majestic peaks and permanent ice fields. They were closing fast on their intended target.

"The homing device is operating perfectly," Ulm said, jabbing a gloved finger at the MI-24's radar screen. On it was a steady fluorescent green blip.

Shirkov looked at the radar, then glared out the cabin's front window. Solid line of snowcapped mountains loomed ahead. "The rebel stronghold," he said through the ship intercom, "appears to be much lower on the mountain than we had been led to believe."

"High or low, it will make no difference to So-man II," Ulm said confidently.

"It will make a difference to the antiaircraft gunners," Shirkov snapped back. "They will have a much easier time shooting us out of the sky."

Ulm was not concerned. There were plenty of expendable gunships along on the mission to absorb any lucky shots the rebels made.

The formation closed ranks as it prepared to make its first pass on the target.

Major Shirkov put his ship into a screaming, high-speed dive. The other gunships followed, dropping well below the line of mountain summits. The advantage of coming out of the sun was seriously weakened by the angle of attack they were forced to assume.

Almost at once the enemy positions opened fire. Flashes of light winked at them from fortified gun emplacements high on the mountainside. The rebel gunners could shoot down at them, against the contrasting backdrop of low clouds.

Over the howl of the MI-24's engine, Ulm and company could hear the chilling, Doppler whine of near misses.

The right-side gunner suddenly shouted into his throat mike, overloading it, his words a rasping screech. A helicopter on his side took a solid hit.

As Shirkov and Ulm turned to look, the gunship in question dropped out of the sky, rotors slowing. The fuselage of the craft began to turn around the pivot point of the dead main rotor. Round and round it spun, black smoke billowing from the cabin. It hit the mountainside and exploded.

In short order, a second, then a third attack helicopter was hit by antiaircraft fire. One blew up in midair; the other plowed headlong into the mountain.

"Damn!" Shirkov growled. He squeezed his throat mike, snarling an order to the rear element of the fleet. "Smash those gun positions! The rest of you, follow me."

Ulm's stomach rebeled as the MI-24 powered out of the steep dive. He refused to give in to nausea. This was the moment he had waited a lifetime for.

"Arm rockets," Shirkov said through the ship-to-ship, flipping a switch on the instrument panel. Confirmation of arming crackled through the MI-24's headsets from the four other Soman II-bearing helicopters.

The pulse of the homing device was strong and clear.

"Lock on," Shirkov said.

Ulm gripped the arms of his chair. Though he strained he could not see the target through the front window. The mountain was too far away to make out more than its most grossly enormous features.

"Fire!" the major said.

The gunship shuddered as its entire pod of rockets launched en masse, leaving a great puff of smoke behind. Shirkov peeled off to the left, giving ground to the gunship on his tail, so that it, too, could launch.

Ulm looked out the side window, following the vapor trails of rockets in flight. Out of the confusion of the mountainside, the cave, a tiny opening some thousand meters distant, appeared to him only at the moment of impact. And then only as a spot of brilliant yellow.

Each gunship in turn fired its missiles.

The flashes of rocket impacts were concentrated in an area the size of a small swimming pool. Yellow flowed down the mountain like a waterfall of daffodils.

The five MI-24s broke off the attack at Shirkov's signal and, along with the rest of the attack group, moved out of range of the mountain batteries. They made lazy circles in formation, giving the deadly gas time to work its way down to the deepest levels of the cave system.

Ulm watched the sweep second hand of his wristwatch like a vulture. When exactly twelve minutes had passed, he said, "Take me back!"

Shirkov did not lead the return to target. It was the troop-carrying helicopters that moved in first. They could not land on the steep mountainside to unload their men, so they hovered over the widest parts of the trail while soldiers in chemwar suits with AKs strapped to their backs slid down ropes deployed from gunship bay doors.

Ulm made his descent in a rescue chair, eyes tightly shut, heart thumping. When he touched ground he was helped out of the chair by chemwar troopers. On shaky legs, he began the short climb down the trail to the cave entrance.

He could see squads of soldiers marching into the broad opening, assault rifles at the ready. Around the cave mouth for a good thirty meters Soman II was splattered high and wide. Sticky yellow dripped from rock to rock.

Excellent shooting, he thought as he stepped to the end of the queue of troopers waiting to enter the stronghold. There seemed to be some kind of holdup at the start of the line. Both impatient and curious, the professor moved out of the queue to see what was happening.

A half dozen of the men about to enter the cave turned suddenly away from the entrance. Three of them dropped after taking a step or two, their legs giving way under them. The rest staggered like drunkards walking straight off the trail, falling headlong off the precipice.

Ulm instinctively stopped breathing. He was already within ten meters of the cave mouth. Yellow was all around him.

Yellow.

He could now see the knot of bodies packed into the front of the cave, boot soles of corpses stacked like cordwood. Then the men in line ahead of him started to drop, cut down as if by an invisible scythe. They dropped where they stood and thrashed, legs kicking frantically.

Ulm didn't know why it was happening but he knew what was making it happen. Soman II. It was killing them all. Still holding his breath, he turned and hurried back up the hill. He only got a few steps before breathing became difficult.

Hypochondria, he told himself. A by-product of an overkeen mind. Keep moving and everything is going to be all right.

His legs went soft in the knees and simultaneously his bowels and bladder emptied. Tears streamed down his face, slobber drooled from his mouth.

It was not hypochondria.

Better than anyone, Ulm knew the effects of nerve-gas poisoning. He collapsed to his side on the trail and could not rise. His whole body quivered with violent spasms. Lost somewhere in the middle of the catalog of symptoms, Dr. Ulm was clear-headed, conscious, terrified. He could not make his lungs draw air; they trembled uselessly in his wildly heaving chest. As his desperation crescendoed, his penis became erect for the first time in decades. Against his will.

It was anticlimax.

A final humiliation as the walls of death swiftly closed in

21

With both hands free, Aziz Khan moved quickly down the mountain. He caught sight of Tajik just as the boy rounded a turn in the trail and disappeared behind a towering cliff. Aziz threw aside all caution and closed the gap in a near spring. When he reached the turn, he stopped short. The bend marked the beginning of a broad V-shaped cut in the mountainside. Tajik walked the trail directly across the V from him, in straight-line distance about fifty meters away. Between them, however, was a chasm that opened onto nothing but the veil of clouds, thousands of meters below. A chill wind howled up through the gap.

Aziz knew if he tried to follow he would be in plain sight. If Tajik was going to run from him, he would run then. And if Aziz waited for the other boy to clear the cut, he would only lose that much more ground. Keeping up with the taller, faster boy seemed more important than the element of surprise.

"Tajik!" Aziz shouted across the gap.

Young Bula froze on the trail, turning to stare over at him.

"Wait for me!"

"No!" came the reply. Tajik waved his black gun. "Stay back!"

Aziz paused. "I found the black box you tried to hide," he said. "We have to talk, Tajik. I want to know what the box was for."

"I hid nothing! Go back, leave me alone."

"I saw you hide it. And I moved it."

"You what?" Tajik said in a voice suddenly shrill. "Where? Where did you move it?"

Aziz did not have a chance to answer. From high above and across the valley from them, Soviet gunships in attack formation power-dived the mountainside. Antiaircraft guns on the summit opened fire. Quickly, three of the helicopters were hit and crashed. There were seventeen more Hinds to follow. Rockets zoomed from the point of the attack wedge. They exploded well up on the mountain.

Aziz saw the yellow gas bloom. His mind made the final connection. "The village!" he cried across the chasm. "My family! It was you!"

Tajik shut his eyes and opened fire with the black gun, spraying 7.62 mm slugs full-auto across the gap.

Aziz threw himself down on his face. Slugs chipped rock above and below him.

When he stopped shooting and opened his eyes, Bula saw the other boy down. Thinking he had hit his target, he broke off the attack and ran on down the trail.

The smaller boy jumped up and pursued. No longer caring about himself, wanting only vengeance, justice for his family.

Tajik could hear the footfalls gaining. He turned and looked back along the stretch of straight trail. He shut his eyes and pinned the AK's trigger as the other boy dashed into view. He cut loose a 10-round burst that went wide to the right, then raced on.

In his panic and haste, he missed one of the trail markers. Instead of climbing above and avoiding a long slide of rubble that lay against the mountainside, he tried to cross it. He was five strides from safety when the face of the slope gave way under him. Screaming, he threw his arms out to grab on to something. The black gun went flying up slope. It landed near the edge of the rubble pile. Tajik clawed at the loose stones, slipping down, down, down the chute. Then his left foot found something solid and his progress toward oblivion stopped.

Aziz stood panting at the verge of the slide. He could see that it ended abruptly five meters below Tajik's position, where the ledge that had caused the pile to accumulate had finally been overwhelmed by its volume. From the edge of the buried shelf, rocks tumbled in a torrent off into space.

"Why?" Aziz shouted down at the sobbing boy. "Why did you do it?"

"The gun," Tajik bawled. "I wanted the gun. I wanted to be a hero."

Aziz stared at the weapon. It was two meters from him. On the deadly slide of rubble.

"Save me!" Tajik begged.

"I cannot," Aziz said, "I have no rope. There is no way."

"Then forgive me!" Tajik cried.

"I cannot," Aziz said. With that, he jumped out onto the pile and grabbed the AK by the sling. The ground slipped away under him as he turned back. He dived for the safety of the trail, thunder rolling at his heels. He heard a scream as he hauled himself up. Aziz looked over his shoulder, squinting against the swirling clouds of dust. The whole heap of rubble had shifted downward.

Tajik was gone.

There was *badal*.

In the sky overhead, another Russian gunship exploded. Aziz felt a warmth next to his heart. With the help of Allah he had deceived the atheist invaders. The mujahedeen would survive, their enemies would be destroyed.

He raised his black gun over his head and shook it; he shouted to the heavens. "*Allah es akbar!*"

22

"Just take the woman!?" Lee fumed. "Hayes, you dirty, low-life..."

Claude laughed. "It's just a joke, Doc," he assured her.

"Maybe not," Barrabas said. He was not smiling.

Lee Hatton glared at the colonel. She swung the muzzle of her AK in his general direction. "I didn't hear that. You didn't say it. You didn't even think it."

"Lighten up, Hatton," Barrabas told her. "We'll play this no different than any other tight spot we've ever been in. If we don't all get out, none of us gets out."

"Then what's all this bull about handing me over to the noble fighters for freedom, justice and the Afghan way?" she demanded.

"It's bull, like you said. But we've got to do something to draw them out. Making them think we're throwing in the towel, or considering it, might do the trick. Liam, get the Greek back here with that LAW."

When O'Toole returned with Nanos, Barrabas told him, "Have Starfoot hold off firing the LAW until he gets a clean shot at the big mouth up there. After he shoots, things are going to happen fast. Stay on your toes."

Nanos nodded and set off again down the canyon.

"Beck, you and Hayes round up as many horses as you can," the colonel said. "Keep low and quiet."

"We're gonna make a run for it, huh?" Liam said.

"First we've got to do some wheeling and dealing," Barrabas told him. He cupped his hands to his mouth and shouted up at the canyon ridge. "We want to talk a trade."

"I am listening," Ahmad Yar shouted back.

"We won't give up our guns or our ammunition," Barrabas said, "but you can have the woman in return for our free passage out of here."

The curt reply came without pause. "We will kill you and take the guns, the bullets and the woman."

"Can you see him?" Barrabas asked Liam and Hatton.

"No," O'Toole said, "but it sounds like he's almost directly above us. A cautious bastard."

"Remember what happened last time I put on a show for these guys?" Lee said. "Maybe if I stood out there in the open and did a burlesque routine?"

"Some other time," Barrabas said.

"*Any* other time," Gunther added.

A few seconds later Beck crab-crawled over to them. "Got eight of the horses, Colonel," he said. "Hayes is holding them behind that big rock. The mules are gone."

"When the LAW hits," Barrabas said, "get Naazmomad over a saddle on his belly quick as you can and then all of us will ride like hell down the canyon. We'll pick up Billy Two and Nanos as we pass."

"And the rebels at the rockfall?" Liam asked.

"We've got enough ammo to take care of them if they try to stop us from breaking out." Barrabas put his hands to his mouth and called up at Ahmad Yar. "All right. We give in. Your terms. We're throwing down our weapons."

The clatter of assorted Kalashnikovs landing on rocks was followed by the appearance in the open of a fully clad and grim-faced Leona Hatton.

"I HATE THE SOUND OF GUNS HITTING THE DIRT," Nanos muttered as the Indian shouldered the team's last LAW.

Billy Two peered through the optical sight, aiming up at the ridge top. "What's the matter—don't you think I can center-ring the creep?"

"Shooting a man with a LAW," the Greek declared, "is like squashing a fly with a bowling ball."

"Oh, looky-looky," the Indian said, grinning.

"What? Can you see him?" Nanos squinted up, shielding his eyes with the edge of his hand. He saw a little black bump on the flat gray line of the ridgetop. The bump had not been there a second or two before. "Holy shit!" Nanos exclaimed. "He is *small*!"

"No sweat."

"If you miss," the Greek went on, "there's no backstop. That flipping rocket is going to fly all the way to Pakistan."

"All of you, stand up!" the bump bellowed down.

"Not you, Alex!" Billy growled out of the corner of his mouth.

"I wasn't going to. Hey, he's coming down."

The bump appeared in silhouette, then descended to a ledge below the ridge line. He moved behind the cover of a rock balanced on the ledge.

"We got your backstop," Starfoot said. "The only question now is which way will the man jump?"

Before Nanos could speculate, the spotting rifle barked. A single 9 mm round whined up and away, pinging off the concealing rock. The rebel leader jumped left.

It was the wrong way.

The LAW whooshed. Its rocket tracked on a draftsman's line straight to Ahmad Yar's midsection. There was a terrific crack and flash as the warhead detonated. Then something dark and limp slid down from the ledge. It wasn't nearly big enough to be the body of a man.

"Just legs," Nanos said as the thing tumbled. "Where's the rest of him?"

"Who the fuck cares?"

The rest of the SOBs arrived thirty seconds after the shot. Billy Two jumped on a riderless horse. Nanos swung up behind Lee Hatton.

The rebels at the rockfall only put up a token resistance to the sudden mounted assault. They had lost their leader and their taste for the job at hand. The SOBs with Barrabas at the point rode over the barrier, firing AKs from the hip. As the mercenaries raced away down the canyon to Pakistan and freedom, there was no deadly flurry of answering fire at their backs. Over the clomp of horses hooves the only sounds the SOBs heard from behind were the soldiers of Allah arguing, yelling at one another at top volume across the chasm.

It was music to their ears.

Nile Barrabas and the
Soldiers of Barrabas are the

SOBs

by Jack Hild

Nile Barrabas is a nervy son of a bitch who
was the last American soldier out of Vietnam
and the first man into a new kind of action. His
warriors, called the Soldiers of Barrabas, have
one very simple ambition: to do what the
Marines can't or won't do. Join the Barrabas
blitz! Each book hits new heights—this is
brawling at its best!

"Nile Barrabas is one tough SOB himself. . . .
A wealth of detail. . . . SOBs does the job!"
—*West Coast Review of Books*

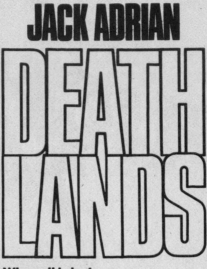

4 FREE BOOKS
1 FREE GIFT
NO RISK
NO OBLIGATION
NO KIDDING